The Geek Girl Squad:

Jade

JASMINE C. CALDWELL

Copyright © 2023 by Jasmine C. Caldwell

Library of Congress Control Number: 2025904793

Edited by Jennifer Herrington

Proofread by Roxana Coumans Book Editing

Cover illustrations by dashwen and Erin Carver

Interior formatted in Atticus

All rights reserved. No part of this publication may be reproduced, stored, or transmitted in any form or by any means, electronic, mechanical, photocopying, recording, scanning, or otherwise without written permission from the publisher. It is illegal to copy this book, post it to a website, or distribute it by any other means without permission. The author does not give consent for this work to be used to train AI.

This novel is entirely a work of fiction. The names, characters, and incidents portrayed in it are the work of the author's imagination. Any resemblance to actual persons, living or dead, events or localities is entirely coincidental.

Designations used by companies to distinguish their products are often claimed as trademarks. All brand names and product names used in this book and on its cover are trade names, service marks, trademarks, and registered trademarks of their respective owners. The publishers and the book are not associated with any product or vendor mentioned in this book. None of the companies referenced within the book have endorsed the book.

Notes from Jasmine

I know, I know, I usually put notes at the end of the book. But this is important information that I want everyone to understand before you get into the last book of the Geek Girl Squad series.

Jade came first. In fact, I wrote the first draft of the scene where Jade and Andrew meet before I even had *names* for all the ladies in the squad.

Back when GGS was nothing but a nebulous concept, I took a break from editing *Roar for Me* to sit down and brainstorm this series' characters. I knew I wanted them to come from all walks of life to better represent the geek community.

Ever hear the myth of Athena's birth? She popped out of Zeus's head, fully grown. That's what happened to me.

I was sitting at my kitchen table when a six-foot-tall black woman with long box braids popped out of my writer brain, shook my hand, and introduced herself as Jade. "By the way, I'm trans."

I was so nervous about writing a trans main character that I nearly changed that aspect before publishing Olivia's story. But I went ahead with it. (Jade's very convincing with that baseball bat.)

Thanks to some amazing authors and YouTubers in the trans community, when it came time to write this book, I felt confident I could do this story justice. I'll save those names for the notes at the end.

So buckle up and prepare for the "saved the best for last" of the Geek Girl Squad series!

XOXO,

Jasmine

Chapter 1

"I WANT TO SPEAK to your manager!"

Jade Aguillard bit the inside of her lip to keep her sanity. "Ma'am, I *am* the manager. We've already remade your drink. There's nothing else we can do."

"Give me a refund! I could have been really sick because of his incompetence."

She sighed. This was the fifth time this month that this Karen (not her real name) had pulled this act. And Jade didn't relish what was about to come next.

"Ma'am, you told him you wanted soy milk. Now you say you're allergic. But the first drink *was* what you ordered. We have had this same issue five times with you and you will not be getting any more free drinks from this establishment."

The customer's pale skin turned bright red, which clashed terribly with her brassy blonde hair. "The hell I won't!"

Jade remained calm, because she knew the patron wanted a rise out of her. "According to store policy, you're banned. Permanently."

"How *dare* you!"

Sigh. "You have thirty seconds before I call the police for trespassing."

The customer huffed and stalked away, past the line that ran right up to the door. Jade shook her black braids and went back to making drinks with her employees as the seventeen-year-old kid that had made the drink came out of the break room. She'd sent him there to protect him from Karen's wrath. As manager, she took on the irate customers threatening to throw beverages. Those kids didn't get paid enough for that shit.

"I'm sorry, Jade."

"It's not your fault, Miguel. She's done this several times." Slowly, the chatter came back to the small cafe, bouncing off the exposed brick wall across from where she stood at the dark wood counter. The green awning outside their window flapped in the breeze as everything returned to normal.

But they hadn't heard the last from "Karen."

A half hour later, the woman stormed in with a cop trailing behind her. Jade's heart pounded. She *couldn't* be serious!

"That's her, officer. She refused to refund my money."

"Ma'am," the officer tipped his hat. "I hate to take up so much of your time when you're clearly busy, but I need to ask you a few questions."

Great. A white woman called the cops on a Black one for simply doing her job. This didn't bode well. Jade sighed and lifted the barrier to the counter, and waved the police officer over to a corner of the cafe. His badge read "Koslowski," and he was slightly shorter than her, so she stooped just a little, unconsciously ceding to his authority. She proceeded to explain everything, in front of the customer, who tried to interject every so often, but he shushed her.

"And that's why she's been banned from the shop, sir."

He raised his pale eyebrows. "Banned?" Then Officer Koslowski turned to the former patron. "Let me get this straight. You have been weaseling free coffee from this cafe after purposely messing up your drink order, and when you were kicked out, you interrupted a police officer on duty to help you trespass?"

Karen stammered and sputtered as he took her by the arms. "You're going to need to come with me to the station." He turned back to Jade. "My apologies, Miss, she won't bother you anymore."

Stunned, Jade didn't move from her spot as the police officer frogmarched the problem customer outside. When the door shut, a cheer erupted from the other customers, and a grin spread out over her face that matched the smiles on her staff.

"Holy crap," said Destinee, her dark eyes wide. "Do you believe that?"

Jade's heart was still pounding. "Let's just be thankful Leanne wasn't here today." The regional manager would have only made things worse.

"For sure." Her smile just about blinded Jade as she turned to the next person in line. "Hi, welcome to The Bean. How can I help you?"

Both registers rang as Jade and her baristas mixed and poured. What could have gone south very easily had become the best workday she'd had at the cafe since her former regional manager, Ben, had been there.

Back when she was still a student at UMD, Ben had hired her for the on-campus branch of The Bean. He'd been the store manager there, and they got along like a house on fire. After finding out she was also into comic books, Marvel especially, the two of them would chat all shift long. Whenever she was scheduled to work with him, she didn't feel like she was working at all.

He got promoted to regional manager the same spring she graduated, bringing her in to manage the Canton branch when their last manager left. While she no longer saw him as regularly as she used to, Ben knew how Jade worked, and they both had similar expectations. This job hadn't been the same since he'd left a year ago. Now Jade could see he'd shielded her from the corporate office's micromanaging. And she had no desire to move up anymore.

Her shift finished, Jade hung up her green apron and visor on their hook, then punched out on the computer. God forbid she actually worked more than forty hours in this hellhole. She clocked out five minutes late exactly once after the blender exploded, and got reamed out by Leanne on the phone the next day. Apparently, they expected her to punch out on time and then go back and clean up the spilled smoothie, unpaid.

Fuck that shit.

Jade cracked her neck as she walked to the bus stop. Summer was hot in Baltimore, but not nearly as muggy as her home state of Louisiana. Still, she was grateful for the cool air conditioning of the Maryland Transit Authority.

In the middle of the afternoon, there weren't too many people that rode this route. So getting back to her apartment took no time at all. The bus shelter was at the end of her block, and her stomach growled as she passed the pizza shop that the squad always ordered from. Garlic, yeast, and herbs flavored the breeze with free advertising. Inside Mason Hollow Apartments, Jade's tired legs carried her up the black metal staircase to her floor. The peeling wallpaper and the stained carpet in need of a scrub no longer fazed her.

The reason she lived here, besides the rent being cheap, was the fact her friends were all there. Well, at least they used to. Olivia had moved into her boyfriend Jake's condo, but for two glorious years the whole squad was together in the same building. They hadn't wanted to separate too far when they left their college campus apartment.

Jade had grown up with four sisters, and while those women no longer recognized her, she had found new ones at the University of Maryland: Olivia, Nadia, Rosie, and Mia. They had bonded over their love of nerdy things and dubbed themselves the Geek Girl Squad, after the Teen Girl Squad from *Homestar Runner*. They were her family, along with Memaw. That was all she needed. And their significant others were basically her in-laws.

Nadia had ended up with Caleb, Jake's best friend, and Rosie had fallen for Matt, Olivia's little brother. Mia reconnected with a girl she knew from her teenage years, and now everyone was… busy. Nadia and Mia split their time between home and their partners' places, and Matt had moved into Rosie's unit. Olivia and Jake came over for game nights, but hosted plenty of them as well, since they had way more space. But the squad was spending less and less time together, and more with their significant others.

Jade hated to admit it, but she was lonely.

She shucked off her shoes at the door, her arches crying out for relief. Then she fell down on her couch with her long legs stretched out. Jade turned her phone off silent for the first moment since she went to bed last night and sent a group text.

Jade: Hey are we gaming this week?

Nadia: That depends on Rosie's schedule.

Rosie: I'm working days, but Matt and I have to travel to his cousin's wedding this weekend.

Olivia: Are we carpooling with you guys? We can split the gas.

Rosie: I'll ask Matt when he gets home from the restaurant.

Mia: Marcia and I are free!

Nadia: So no D&D, but we could do something else?

Jade: Sounds good.

It was certainly better than sitting around by herself.

Mia: We should decide what we're doing for Jade's birthday. It's the week after next.

Jade: I don't need anything.

Nadia: Does not compute.

Olivia: Don't make us plan a surprise party!

Jade laughed. That didn't sound so bad.

Mia: Just think about it, and when we get together we'll discuss, okay? You only turn twenty-five once!

She shook her head even though her friend couldn't see her, then shuffled to her kitchen to figure out dinner before her aching feet petrified on the couch.

Lunchtime at the offices above the Neon Unicorn meant Andrew Monroe had time to himself. Once he'd finished his sandwich and chips, he leaned back in his leather desk chair and pulled out the latest issue of *Immortal X-Men* he had bought at the comic shop a few blocks away. He had always felt an affinity with the mutants; growing up biracial, he'd heard all kinds of insults. People didn't expect to see freckles across a wide nose, or auburn dreadlocks.

Too bad his genes hadn't come with some kind of superpower, like his favorite heroes.

Just as he was about to open the book, his door opened. "Knock, knock! Guess who?"

Internally, Andrew groaned. "Aiden, shouldn't you still be sleeping for your shift tonight?"

His mirror image sashayed into his office. Well, they were identical from the neck up, and they had the same basic height and build. But where Andrew liked conservative work clothes, Aiden's style was more casual.

A purple fedora matched his twin brother's African-print t-shirt, along with his high-top sneakers. At least he was wearing jeans to the office, even if they were white and skin-tight, instead of hot pants.

Andrew didn't need to see *that* again.

"I can sleep when I'm dead. Or when Jeffrey comes over." He sat his ass on Andrew's desk and waggled his eyebrows.

"I highly doubt you get any rest when your new boyfriend is there with you."

Aiden lifted one shoulder and batted his eyelashes in faux innocence. "Whatever do you mean?"

He rolled his eyes at his twin's antics. "What did you need so badly that you had to interrupt my lunch?"

"Can you work my security shift this weekend? Pleeeeeease?" Andrew suppressed a groan as his brother begged. "Jeffrey wants me to go to Philadelphia with him. Apparently there's some big reunion and I have to meet the parents." Aiden shuddered.

As much as he hated the idea of working an entire night at the club, he rejoiced over his twin being serious enough about someone to introduce them to the family. Aiden could be flighty, but he seemed to be settling down now that they were in their thirties. And Jeffrey sounded like a great guy; Andrew liked what he'd heard.

"Are you bringing him to Sunday dinner soon?"

He didn't miss Aiden's wince. "I guess I have to, huh?"

"It'd be a lot easier than driving to another state. You could have done it already." Andrew hesitated before hauling out the big guns. "It hardly seems fair to Mom and Dad that you're seeing his family first when you both live here."

Aiden sighed. "We're coming home on Sunday, so we'll make it then."

"Deal." Andrew knew he was getting the shit end of the stick here, but *he* was the one Mom kept whining to about not meeting Aiden's boyfriend yet.

"Just try not to let her embarrass me?"

"I'll do my best, and I'm sure you'd do the same for me."

"Eventually, you'll bring someone home for the first time and find out exactly how awful this is."

Not the way Andrew was progressing, he wouldn't. Nobody that he'd met in years had stuck around. And he was starting to feel that at his age, if he hadn't found a partner by now, then he wasn't going to.

"You're the best, Bro!" Aiden hopped off the desk and gave him a smacking kiss on the cheek, despite Andrew's grimace. He wiped off his face as his twin ran out of the room. "I owe you!"

Damn right he did.

Sighing, Andrew picked the comic book back up and was on the first page when someone else came to the door.

"Hey boss."

Ember was one of his bartenders, plus his best friend from college. Her burgundy hair hung in a braid down her sun-tanned shoulder, a fresh shave on the side of her head. A gold nose ring glinted from her septum.

"Hey Ember. You know you don't have to call me that, right?"

"But you're my boss here. I wouldn't want everyone else thinking I'm getting special treatment just 'cause I saw you puke your guts out when you turned twenty-one," she said with a grin.

Andrew snorted. "Stop reminding me. What's up?"

Ember sighed. "Another order got messed up. They dropped off two cases of the vodka and no tequila."

So much for Tequila Tuesdays. "Alright, I'll tell Aiden to pull the social media campaign. Run a special on vodka and cranberry juice. It's not like we won't use the stock. And I'll have a talk with the supplier."

"When are you going to get some help in here? I'm worried about you two." Her tone changed to that of his friend, and not his employee. "I don't want to see you burn out."

"I'll try, but who knows when we'd find the time to even put out an ad, much less hire anybody." Hiring and training took hours he didn't have, because he was so busy putting out fires at the club.

And now he was working for Aiden on Saturday night, when he was supposed to balance the books.

"You need some kind of office manager. I'll see if anyone I know can help."

"Sounds good." Ember left, and his lunch was nearly over. Damn it, that reminded him he *still* had to put out the schedule for the next two weeks. The employees had been incredibly patient, but he had promised them it would be out in time for them to make their plans.

But he had a meeting to go to first.

He pulled his laptop off his desk and strode to Aiden's office, which he rarely used despite being in charge of marketing *and* security. His twin was inside with their mother, Monica. She was a silent partner in their business, having run a successful one herself, and they had a weekly meeting where they talked shop with her. Her advice had been priceless.

When they finally got done going through the changes to the social media, and the supplier issues, his mom turned and repeated everything Ember had said to him, almost verbatim. "You need an office manager so you can focus on the bigger tasks."

"Sure, we'll hire one in our spare time." She balked at his sarcasm, so he backpedaled a bit. It wasn't her fault he was on edge lately. "I promise. Just as soon as things calm down around here, Mom." She nodded, and they continued with the meeting. Hopefully that was the last he'd have to hear about it for now.

Chapter 2

That night, Jade's long fingers typed haltingly away at yet another cover letter as she struggled to keep her eyes in focus. Job hunting sucked. Her income was so low her monthly student loan payments were zero. But that meant that the loan company tacked the interest she accrued onto the principal balance every year. And she knew if the situation didn't change soon, she was going to end up owing more than she could ever repay. Thank goodness she had only borrowed enough for room and board.

Between Memaw's limited income and her grades, Jade had managed to get tuition covered with scholarships. She sighed, taking a break and rolling her wrist around to ease the tension. Damn, she missed her grandmother. It was almost time for their standing weekly phone call, though, so Jade got right back to work. She wanted to get another application finished before Memaw called.

She had been looking for months. Sure, she'd only just told Mia about it. But the fact was that Jade couldn't manage The Bean much longer without committing murder. Her supervisor was out to get her. Most likely, Leanne *wanted* her to quit—the old Southern belle hated having a trans woman of color in charge of one of her coffee shops. Her sneers had made that clear from the very beginning.

The previous regional manager, who had promoted Jade and then left, had been a total sweetheart. However, Jade didn't dare leave before she had something else lined up. Hopefully, a job that would pay more than her basic needs.

Mia's rewrites had helped her resume, but she still had to do the actual legwork of applying. And every company wanted her to sign up for an account on their talent network. Which meant re-entering her information each time she applied for a position, even though it was already on the document she'd uploaded.

Not that it was especially long.

Olivia had convinced her to print off all her old projects from college that had received good marks and helped her combine them into a portfolio she could take on interviews. She had a digital file as well that once in a while she could upload to a website as part of her application. So far, all she'd heard in response were automatic emails that said her applications had been accepted and the hiring department would be in touch.

Finally, her phone rang. She picked up without taking her weary eyes off her computer screen.

"Hello?"

"Jade baby, where y'at?"

She couldn't help the grin that spread across her face at Memaw's New Orleans greeting, and answered in kind. "I'm awrite, Memaw. How are you?"

"When you gonna come visit your old Memaw, huh?"

"I want to, so bad. But this dam—darn coffee shop barely covers my bills." Whew. She'd caught herself before swearing at her grandmother.

"I know, child. I'm just messin' with ya. Tell me what all is going on, now."

It was the same conversation they had every week. Like clockwork, Memaw would call so Jade could catch her up on her life up in Baltimore. She'd told her all about how

Mia had reconnected with a girl she'd known as a teen and fallen in love.

"Marcia practically lives here now, and Mia's mentioned moving to a larger place. They want space for Marcia's siblings to stay with them."

"That's so sweet. Speaking of visitin'…"

Jade chuckled ruefully as she cut Memaw off. "I promise I will come visit you once I find a new job. Plane ticket prices go up every year." She'd love to go back home to Louisiana to see Memaw again. Her grandmother wasn't able to travel any longer, and she hadn't seen her since graduation.

"Yes, I know. I'd send you the money myself, but the doctors are getting just as expensive."

What the hell? Her grandmother wouldn't see a doctor — she'd rather use her home remedies. Unless… her life depended on it.

Instantly, Jade was on high alert. "Memaw, what's wrong? What aren't you telling me?"

"Hush, baby. If you needed to know something, I'd tell you."

Jade's brows furrowed, but she didn't call her grandmother out for dodging her question. "You promise?"

"I swear on our ancestors. Everything is gonna be just fine."

Jade finished the conversation in a daze. Hanging up, she went back to her job search. It wasn't like Memaw to keep secrets from her. Ever since she came out at sixteen, it had been her and Lou Ellen Aguillard against the world. Her grandmother had welcomed her into her home, filed for guardianship, and even got her name changed on her birth certificate. She'd taken Jade to the doctors faithfully so she could get the hormone treatments she needed to feel comfortable in her own ebony skin. But Memaw didn't trust western medicine and would rather visit her fellow Voodoo healer friends when illness struck her. She would have to be nearly at death's door to be visiting a physician. Yet she sounded perfectly fine on the phone.

What could she be trying to protect Jade from?

Then, an alert showed up at the bottom of the webpage. "New jobs posted! Refresh now!" Sighing, she did as the site suggested, and startled when she saw the latest listing for an office manager, listed just seconds ago.

Office Manager Wanted

> **Experienced manager wanted for up-and-coming night club in the Baltimore area. Needed to oversee daily activities and schedule of club staff to ensure efficient operations and adequate coverage. Also, will manage record-keeping, maintenance services, and technical support as needed. Coordinate resources to troubleshoot and determine the best solutions. The ideal candidate is a problem solver, self-motivated, and can work independently. Bachelor's degree required. Candidate must be open-minded regarding the LGBTQIA+ community, but does not need to be a member. We are an equal opportunity employer...**

Jade didn't bother to read the bit the employer included about valuing diversity in the workplace. She was sold. This had energized her better than the triple-shot espressos she made so often at The Bean. Her fingers flew across the keyboard as she typed what had to be the most important cover letter of her life. She checked it over three times before deciding it was good and clicking on the 'Apply Now' button. As her resume and portfolio disappeared into the ether, she clenched her fists, closed her eyes, and prayed to all of Memaw's Voodoo deities she could recall for this to work out.

It was everything she'd dreamed of.

Andrew was going to lose his mind. Or Ember and the other bartenders would kill him. Either way, he wasn't long for this world.

The only method to make the schedule function with Dru out for six months was for everyone to pitch in twice as many hours. Especially with the crowds The Neon Unicorn had been drawing lately, as word of the club spread. And they hadn't given him much notice that they were leaving to film a movie.

He better go down there and explain himself.

Taking the schedules off the printer, he marched down the stairs to the bar, where Ember and Colin were stocking for the upcoming night.

"Hey guys, bad news." Andrew slapped the schedule down on the black lacquered surface. "Dru got a spot in a film and they're going to be out for six months. Which means I have to hire someone else..."

"And we have to pick up the slack 'til you find them." Ember crossed her arms on the bar and leaned over. "No sweat, boss. Dru was so excited about the role. We can handle it till you bring in a temp. And by the time Dru's back, we'll probably need to keep the new one, anyway."

Andrew sighed, ignoring the ivory cleavage she was flashing at him. He knew she only did it for tips, despite his mom wondering out loud many times why they hadn't dated. She thought they'd make beautiful babies. But he'd never had those kinds of feelings towards Ember, and she didn't feel that way for *any*one.

"Bigger tip share, anyway," Colin said.

"You know it."

"Thanks guys." Andrew rubbed his temples. "I'll find someone just as soon as I can, so this doesn't drag on too long."

"Of course you will." Ember's vote of confidence relaxed him. "Now get out of here. You've been working nine hours. Go home and eat."

"I already work with my mom. I don't need a second one." He teased her. "See you guys later."

"Good night!"

Back in his apartment, he loosened his collar and headed to the bedroom. Andrew's stomach was growling as he passed the open living and kitchen space, but he wanted to change clothes first. He slipped the tie and white collared shirt off, then put his loafers carefully in their place on the organizer. His dress pants were next, and then he changed into his gym shorts and a workout tank. Once he'd switched his socks and slid his running shoes on, he went out to the kitchen and took a frozen dinner out of the freezer. There was no point cooking for just himself.

The meal reheated in five minutes, and he stood at his island to consume it. Then he filled his water bottle, grabbed his phone, earbuds, and his key, and strode into the hall.

He worked out three times a week in the building's gym on the second floor, mirrored walls reflecting all his hard work back at him. It was a modern building that he got into when he had his 'big kid' — and soul-sucking — accounting job. He'd saved for a long time to start this club with his brother, even saving a few years of bills before making the leap. It had been worth it. No longer a slave to the corporate mindset, he wore his russet-colored locs with no hassle.

Aerosmith pumped through the speaker in the corner, and he stretched to "Dude Looks Like A Lady" before getting sick of it and putting his own music in his ears. Andrew went through all his various weight reps and then hit the treadmill for a run.

No human interaction.

As he walked back to his apartment, his shirt soaked with sweat, he wondered if he needed to get out more. Aiden often told him as much. His twin loved to try talking him into meeting people; whether it was a night on the town in college, or thinly veiled attempts to test the waters with Jeffrey's friends. Andrew had done the casual dating thing in his twenties, but now folks his age wanted to settle down. They were looking for a commitment. And he'd never be able to give someone that, because he didn't trust his heart with anyone.

It still bore the scars from the last time he gave it away. He couldn't survive that again.

"So, what do you want for your birthday?" Mia didn't pull any punches as soon as they sat around Nadia's table with their pizza in hand.

"A new job," Jade retorted as she bit off her slice of heaven and chewed.

Mia recognized her sarcasm easily and smirked. "I think you'd hate that if I actually did it."

Jade pretended to consider it, then nodded. "Seriously, I don't need anything."

"We have to do *some*thing!" Nadia cried. "We've done stuff for everyone else's birthday. Why not yours?"

I'm nothing special, was her immediate thought. But she knew saying that wouldn't fly with her squad.

"I just want to hang out with you guys. Have some fun."

Marcia, who'd tagged along to girls' night with Mia, swallowed her bite and spoke. "Have you seen that new gay club? The Neon Unicorn?"

"I've heard of it." Jade shifted in her seat. "Actually, I applied for a job there. Apparently, they need an office manager."

Mia's brown eyes nearly popped out of her head. "Oh my God, that sounds perfect for you!"

Nadia clapped her hands. "*That's* what we should do! We should scope this club out."

Jade furrowed her brows. "What do you mean?"

"It's research. We can go out for your birthday and see what this place is like. That way, you get a fun night out *and* you'll know ahead of time if this business is somewhere you want to work." Nadia tightened the elastic surrounding her long chestnut hair, green eyes sparkling. "Employers are far more impressed in interviews if you're familiar with their business."

That made total sense, and Jade nodded along. Mia had a sneaky smirk on her face as she looked at Nadia.

"But you still need to pick a present or something."

Ugh, what could she say? "A foot massage? My feet will be so glad when I leave The Bean."

"Pedicure it is!" Mia clapped.

Jade sighed. She knew better than to argue. "Alright."

"We'll get all dolled up and go out to the club! Ooh, I bet I can find a limo." Mia's blonde hair curtained around her phone, her fingers flying across the screen.

"No limos, please?"

"But some of them come with bottle service!"

Nadia pushed her black-framed glasses back up. "Mia, she wants to dance and have a good time, not get white-girl-wasted."

Mia raised her head and scowled. "What are you tryin' to say, Nadia?"

"You're cute when you're trashed, *mi amor*." Marcia chuckled.

Jade laughed. Mia did make an adorable drunk. Like Tinkerbell without wings.

Nadia shook her head. "My point was, I think she prefers to remember the night."

"Y'all are no fun. So no bottle service. But how are we going to get there if we all want to drink?" Mia pouted, her joy being stolen. "Rideshares aren't necessarily reliable."

"Limos are expensive. I don't need that." Jade shifted in her seat.

"Oh fine, how about a town car?"

"Okay," Jade relented. Mia took any chance she could to spoil people. For her own birthday, she'd treated the squad to a spa day and then a night at a club — with bottle service.

"So yes town car, no bottle service... I guess we're letting the guys at the club buy you drinks?"

Jade snorted. "The guys at the club will probably be more interested in each other. Y'all can buy me drinks instead of presents. Heaven knows they'll be pricey enough."

"True story."

Chapter 3

BASS BEATS THUMPED so loud Jade could feel them in her chest. Her braids swung down her back in a high ponytail. A slinky silver halter dress reflected the rainbow of lights bouncing around the dance floor. She strutted in proudly, "Birthday Girl" spelled out in rhinestones on the tiara from her friends and her silver heels clicking against the tile. At a straight club, Jade would cling to her squad to keep the strange bodies from crowding her. But at The Neon Unicorn, those bodies were her people. Pride banners of all stripes hung from the ceiling, loudly declaring all welcome. She linked arms with Mia, since this was her place, too. Nadia, Olivia, and Rosie trailed close behind them.

"We need some birthday cake shots!" Nadia shouted to be heard over the music, pointing the girls toward the bar. "This round's on me!"

Jade let out a whoop as they sought an opening in the crowd around the counter. Nadia got in first. She spoke to the bartender and handed over her card. The barkeep nodded her half-shaved head and disappeared to run the card. When she returned, she delivered five shots and her card on a small tray.

Nadia led them to a high-top table by the corner that had just opened up. Each girl raised a shot glass. "To Jade! Happy birthday!" The other four members of her squad said in unison. Jade's grin was a mile wide as they all clinked their glasses in the middle, then poured the sweet liquor down the hatch.

"Thanks, guys. It means so much to me for you to come here."

"Of course!" Olivia said as Nadia took their glasses back to the bar. "I'm honestly surprised you hadn't told us about it before."

Jade had heard about The Neon Unicorn when it opened, but hadn't had the guts to enter. In hindsight, she could have asked Mia to go with her before, but it meant everything to have her straight friends support her. And now, with her applying for the job here, she had finally gotten the courage to check it out.

"You three just have to worry about girls hitting on you now," laughed Mia.

"I can't decide if Jake would like that or not." Olivia shook her blonde space buns. Jade had specifically requested a girls' night out, so the boys hadn't come along. Jake, Caleb, and Matt were probably playing video games and enjoying some quality bro time. Mia's girlfriend couldn't join because she had a late appointment.

"I tell you what," Rosie suggested to Olivia. "We'll act like we're together, then you don't have to worry."

"Worry about what?" Nadia came back to the table. They had to yell just to have the conversation.

"Getting hit on," Mia said. "I'll pretend to be with you so we can protect each other."

"Alright. But Caleb might get jealous."

"Not as jealous as if some pushy chick stuck her tongue down your throat." Jade had read some ridiculous stories in online forums, and there wasn't always alcohol involved.

"Point taken." Nadia lifted her hands in surrender. "So, are we gonna dance or what?"

"Hell yes, sugar!" Jade led her friends to the center of the floor.

The club heated up as the night wore on. Jade and her girls were in the zone. As the last single member of the Geek Girl Squad, Jade was looking around at the arm candy. Most of the guys were coupled up with other men, but she saw a few dancing with women. Apparently you never knew at The Neon Unicorn.

Snide laughter and whooping erupted from a booth in the corner. Ugh, the worst kind of group. Creeps who harassed ladies at heterosexual bars sometimes went to gay clubs, because straight women often came here to get away from them. Jade turned back to her friends and kept grooving.

Across the club, she spied what Memaw would call a "tall drink of water." She couldn't make out his features, but he had dreadlocks pulled back at the base of his neck. A black button-down shirt encased wide shoulders, partially open at his pale throat. He wasn't fooling around with anyone, just watching. And when his eyes landed on her, that piercing gaze drove an arrow into her soul. She sent the Adonis a sultry smile, and to her surprise, his lips quirked up at one side in response. Her knees about turned to jelly at his sexy smolder. She was so busy checking him out, she didn't realize someone else was walking up behind her until she felt them grinding on her.

Some dude-bro in a green and white striped polo from the creeper booth was practically humping her ass, and he almost had to go on tiptoes to do it. Jade let out a groan of disgust and stopped her shimmying.

"Back off, buster."

His ears must not be working. She'd certainly been loud enough for him to hear. She put her hand on his shoulder and pushed him away. "I said, back off!"

That got his attention. "Why'd you come here if you don't want to dance?"

"Not with you!"

"Oh, I see how it is. I'll just watch you dance with your girls." He winked suggestively, but didn't move. As Jade was about to take the asshole to task, Adonis swooped in and started grinding on dude-bro's ass. Dude-bro flipped right out at him.

"What the fucking hell, man?!"

Adonis leaned towards him and said, "Why are you at the Neon Unicorn if you don't want to dance?" Dude-bro, his name was probably Chad, sputtered and bolted for his buddies in the corner booth.

Her savior looked up at Jade and spoke in her ear. "Are you alright, miss?" His deep voice was smooth like velvet and good whiskey. She was several inches taller than him in her shoes, but he didn't seem to notice.

"I'm fine, thank you. But you didn't have to come over just to rescue me."

"I was coming this way, anyway." Warm gray eyes stared into hers as he held out his hand. This close, she could see the freckles across his wide nose; and his dreadlocks were lighter than she expected. "I'm Andrew."

"Jade." She put her ebony palm in his and her heart went pitter-patter when he raised it to his lips.

He glanced up at the tiara on her head. "Happy birthday." His hand dropped hers, and she mourned the loss. "Can I buy you a drink?"

"Uh, sure. Let me tell my friends real quick." She held up a finger and leaned over her shoulder to speak into Mia's ear. She looked from Jade to Andrew, then nodded in understanding. He offered his palm again and led her to the bar, the crowd parting like the Red Sea for them. As if by magic, two stools at the end were open. Who *was* this guy?

"Ember, I'll have the usual," He addressed the bartender when she came over. "And what would you like?"

"I'll take a Jack and Coke, please." Jade took this time to study his features closer in the light over the bar. He was handsome, but he looked older than her by at least five years. She could see the laugh lines starting around those thick, pillowy lips. He'd rolled his sleeves up to his elbows, and she caught a small tattoo of Celtic knotwork inside his forearm.

"It's your twenty-first birthday, isn't it?" Andrew leaned over.

Jade laughed. "No, no. That was a while ago."

He gave her a wide smile, and she could have sworn angels were singing on high. "So you're twenty-two?"

She batted her eyelashes at him. "Don't you know it's rude to ask a lady's age?"

He laid a hand over his heart as their drinks appeared in front of them. "I'm so sorry. My mother would be ashamed of me. I only asked because they like to sing if someone's turning twenty-one."

Jade waved the thought away. "That's unnecessary. If they made a big deal out of it, I'd never come back."

"Well, I can't have that."

Ember rushed to their end of the bar, worry on her face. "Andrew, Brian has a situation at the door."

"Shit. I'll be right there."

Nodding, Ember retreated to serve other patrons.

"Do you work here?"

"Yeah..." Andrew rubbed the bridge of his nose as if he were thinking. He glanced at the bartender, who wasn't watching them. Then he fished a pen and a card out of his pocket. Scribbling on the back of it, he handed it to Jade. "I don't normally do this, but this is my cell. Text me and we can meet up sometime. When I'm off the clock."

Jade laid a hand on his arm before he ran off. "Thanks for the rescue, and the drink."

"My pleasure." He gave her that grin again, then his face grew serious. "Get home safe."

She nodded at his retreating back, then fanned herself with the card as she finished her beverage. Good Lord, he was hot! Wait until the girls heard about this.

Andrew groaned when his cell rang, waking him from a well-deserved morning of sleep. One look at the clock, and he realized it was noon. He picked up the phone without looking at the caller id. "It's Raining Men" had told him who it was.

"That is the last time I work an evening shift for you, Brother. I'm too old for this shit," Andrew choked out. He cleared his throat, rough with sleep.

Aiden cackled. "Come on, old man, those four minutes don't mean that much. I do just fine."

"*You* are the night owl. *I* am the early bird." Andrew stretched as he sat up in bed and rubbed a hand down his face before he remembered the fight. The pressure on his chin made him wince. "Don't tell me you're not coming home today. I can't take another shift of douchebags trying to cause trouble."

"Yeah, Ember texted me last night and told me what happened. You going to have a black eye for dinner?"

He rose and checked the mirror. "Nope, but I've got a lovely bruise starting on my jaw."

"You banned him, right?"

"That was why he hit me."

"Ugh. I hate people sometimes."

Andrew didn't want to dwell on the near-brawl in their club. "So you're really bringing Jeffrey home to meet our parents tonight?" Sunday dinner was a family tradition that the twins never missed.

"Hey, I promised. And I'm counting on you to keep Mom away from the photo albums."

"I'll do my best to spoil her fun." Andrew padded barefoot to his kitchen for an ice pack.

"Ember told me something else about last night. You bought a patron a drink?"

Here it came. Why couldn't Ember keep her mouth shut? "I had to get a douchebag off her when he wouldn't take a hint. And it was her birthday. I didn't want her evening ruined."

"Uh-huh." Aiden wasn't buying it. "What did she look like?"

Andrew let his mind wander to the best part of his shift. "Tall, black braids, dark skin, and a dress that reminded me of liquid mercury."

"Did the birthday girl give you a name?" Aiden chuckled, teasing.

Andrew wasn't awake enough to resent it. "Jade." He loved the delicious way it rolled off his tongue. She'd resembled an African moon goddess with her silver eyeshadow and plum lips.

"Tell me you got her number. I haven't heard about you talking to anybody in *ages*."

"No, we didn't have a lot of time before that issue at the door." That reminded Andrew to put an ice pack on his sore jaw. He rummaged through his freezer. "Besides, didn't we agree no dating patrons?"

Or in his case, not seeing anyone. Not that he was going to tell his twin that.

Aiden snorted over the phone. "That was your idea; *I* think it's terrible. We're in business specifically to attract our type of people, so not dating anybody that comes to the club doesn't make sense."

"It still seems weird." Andrew knew his brother was right. But "don't shit where you eat" had been ingrained in him from years in the corporate world. At least he usually worked days in the office, handling things behind the scenes. He had no intention of working the Unicorn while it was open again.

"Agree to disagree. Anyway, I'll see you at dinner, twin!"

Andrew popped two Tylenol and pressed the ice pack for his lunch bag to his jaw. Standing at his kitchen counter in his boxers, he navigated to his texts, hoping Jade had texted. He could never resist Jade's pull, but he couldn't offer her forever. But he had no new messages from unknown numbers. He tried not to be too disappointed. The day was still young.

❦

"You need to text him!" Nadia stood in her apartment, hands on her hips.

"I just want to focus on this interview right now. Besides, aren't you supposed to make them sweat three days?"

Nadia scoffed. "I don't buy that. If you're interested, at least message and give him your number. You can wait till after the interview to go on a date."

"I'll text him after we do these practice questions again." When she'd gotten the call Friday afternoon from the owner of The Neon Unicorn to come in for a meeting, she had squealed so loud Nadia had heard her two doors down. If things went well tomorrow, she and Andrew would be coworkers and would hopefully get to see each other a lot more.

"You're ready, Jade. I promise. Although when they ask if you have questions, I would suggest you find out if they have a 'no fraternization' policy."

That was a good point that Jade hadn't thought of. "Shit, I might not be allowed to date him if I work there."

"Chances are a nightclub will be pretty lax about those kinds of things, but it can't hurt to be upfront."

"True."

Nadia still stood there, tapping her foot. "So?"

"So, what?"

She gestured at Jade's phone sitting on the coffee table. "Aren't you going to text him?"

Jade sighed. "I don't know."

"Clearly you were into him. You left so fast, I didn't even realize you told someone where you'd be. Mia had to restrain me from kicking everyone's ass in that club to find you."

How could she explain it to Nadia, who'd never had to tell a guy she *really* wasn't like other girls?

"Can I trust he doesn't do this every weekend? Or do you think that was a line?"

"All you can do is take what he said at face value. Plus, I feel if he was used to it, he wouldn't have hesitated, right? You told us he looked at the bartender before he gave you the card."

But that could have been for show. "He works there. He had a vested interest in my night not being ruined."

Not that it would have been, but the thought was nice.

"You'll never know whether he's interested if you don't text him." Nadia said in a singsong voice, then stood and hugged her. "I better head back to my place. I have to prep my lunches for the week."

"Thanks for the help, and the pep talk."

"Anytime. Remember, this is your job. You just need them to realize that." Nadia squeezed Jade's shoulder and let herself out.

Jade snorted and sat down on her couch. As far as the interview went, she was as prepared as possible. She'd pressed her suit and blouse, planned her bus trip out, and laid her earrings and makeup out on her dresser. She twirled the black card around in her fingers. Her nails were still silver from her visit to the salon with Mia, who'd upgraded her to a mani-pedi despite her protests. Sighing, she tossed the card back onto the coffee table.

Last night was this perfect moment in time, where a guy bought her a drink at a nightclub and everything felt so normal. She couldn't bring herself to shatter it. Because if they met up, it would break. If they dated, it could end badly. Sure, he worked at a queer club, but that didn't mean he himself was. And the darkness of the room would have hidden her prominent Adam's apple, a telltale sign if you knew to look for it. For all he realized, she was a straight cisgender girl, and she'd learned that the chances of guys being into girls with extra parts were slim to none.

Years before, as a transitioning teen, Jade dreamed of getting gender reassignment surgery. But the insurance wouldn't cover it, and the cost put it so far out of reach it was ludicrous. For the first time in ages, the thought flitted across her mind that she could go after him once she had GRS. Then she shook her head and tucked her braids up into her satin sleep cap. Jade had long ago accepted that love wasn't in the cards for her, because she didn't fit into a nice, neat box. She would be content with her squad. They were much better friends than she'd ever imagined.

Decision made. She wouldn't text him. She would hold last night in her heart like a snow globe and bring it out when she needed some joy.

Chapter 4

Jade strode down the block to The Neon Unicorn in her shorter, more comfortable dress shoes. At six feet tall, she didn't wear high heels often. The silver stilettos on Saturday night had been the exception.

Restaurants and bars accepted deliveries from trucks parked on the sidewalk. She dodged a guy toting a keg on a dolly as she slipped into the now unguarded front door of The Neon Unicorn, its light-up logo dark in the window.

Her instructions said to ask for Monica, but as she strode into the building, she didn't see anyone. "Hello?"

A short, burly fellow came around the corner, carrying a case of something. "Can I help you?"

"I have a meeting with Monica," she explained as he hefted the alcohol onto the bar. He dusted off his hands and waved her forward.

"Follow me."

Her heels clacked on the black floor, the bright overhead lights giving the club an eerie, empty vibe, as though it wasn't meant to be seen like this.

When he opened a door at the end of a hallway, the contrast struck her immediately as she followed him up the stairs. White walls, blue commercial carpet... It looked like any office out of a television show. An entire wall of windows let in the sunlight.

The fair-haired barback pointed down the hall. "The conference room is the third door on the right."

"Thanks," her voice trailed off as he ran back downstairs. Jade shook herself. The man had a job to do, and it clearly wasn't showing people around.

She glided softly in the direction he indicated. The door was open, but she knocked anyway.

"Come in!" called a cheerful voice. Jade entered to see an older woman, with pale ivory skin and light red hair fringed with white at the temples, in a floral-print blouse and slacks, sitting at a conference table. "You must be Jade! Welcome, I'm Monica."

"Hi, Monica." Jade put on her best smile and extended her hand to shake the owner's. "Thanks for meeting with me."

"Believe me, the pleasure is all mine."

It was more of a pleasant chat than an interview. Monica flipped through her portfolio, impressed with her projects from college. Jade told stories about her experiences managing The Bean, and before she knew it, an hour had flown by. Monica wrapped their meeting up, and Jade nearly forgot to question her about dating when she asked, "Do you have questions for me?"

"Just one," she started. "I was here Saturday night, and a guy — I think he works security — gave me his number." She tried to contain her squirming. "I wanted to know if that would be a problem."

Monica shook her head. "It's difficult to tell what anyone around here is supposed to be doing. We're so short-handed that everyone does a little of everything at the moment." But her smile was reassuring. "But there's no hard and fast policy against it; just try to keep things professional on the clock, yeah?"

"Not a problem." Especially since Jade had no intention of running into him again. But Nadia had been adamant over the text this morning that she ask no matter what. As her friend had put it, "What if someone else interests you? It's best to know ahead of time."

"Well, if that's everything, then I think I just have to ask when you can start."

"I'd have to give my current place two weeks' notice, that's all." Not that Leanne deserved it. But since The Bean was the only job Jade had since graduating, she needed to keep it on her resume.

"You should do that then." Monica grinned. "We need you, stat."

Back on the street in a daze, Jade floated down the sidewalk towards the bus shelter. The wage was far better than she'd imagined, so she hadn't bothered to negotiate. Health insurance, dental, a 401k... she was in shock. She emailed Leanne her official resignation as she waited for her ride, then opened the group chat with the squad. All she said was,

Jade: I got the job!

Andrew puzzled over the latest expense report. Who had made a purchase at the computer store of that amount without running it by him first?

A quick phone call to the shop in question had him dialing his mother. She picked up right away.

"Hello, Andrew. This is a pleasant surprise."

He snorted. "This is a business call, Mom. Why did you make such a big electronics purchase before consulting me?"

"Am I not an equal partner in this club?"

Andrew pinched the bridge of his nose. "Yes, of course, Mom, but you said you wanted to be the silent partner. What's going on?"

"I hired an office manager."

His world came to a stop. "You what?"

"You said you were too busy, and you clearly need help. So I put out the ad and hired someone myself. She'll require a computer to do her job."

"What will she be doing?"

"She will handle inventory orders, scheduling, everything that bogs you down now and keeps you from the big picture stuff."

Sighing, he had to admit she'd been right to do it. But going behind his back like that pissed him off.

"Fine. But next time talk to me and Aiden before you make a move like this, okay? It's not fair to blindside us."

"I'm sorry I did this on my own, but I didn't see much choice what with how busy you've been. It won't happen again." She sounded sufficiently contrite.

"When does she start?"

"She has to give her current place two weeks' notice, but I wanted to order the computer so it's ready for her."

He nodded, though she couldn't see that over the phone. "Alright. Hey, since you're into hiring people, think you can find us a long-term temp bartender for while Dru is out?"

Mom laughed. "Sure, just leave it to me."

Andrew grinned as they said their goodbyes. At least she was willing to help, unlike some silent partners he'd heard about. Speaking of silence.... he glanced over his phone one last time but knew it was futile. His Saturday night goddess hadn't sent him a single word.

He shoved his cell in a drawer and went back to the accounting program, wishing he'd asked for her number instead of rushing off that night. Clearly, she wasn't interested. He would just have to forget her.

But he knew that night, when the moon shone into his bedroom, that she'd visit in his dreams again.

The last two weeks hadn't gone by fast enough. Jade was slinging drinks towards the end of her final shift. The staff had gotten her a cake, and she had cried when she read their card, but the one dark spot on the day was *Leanne* showing up. Apparently she hadn't found a replacement manager yet, and she was going to be running the store until she did.

Jade hated that she was leaving her team in such an awful situation.

"These aren't supposed to be on that side of the counter!" Leanne moved the pitchers to the other side of the blenders, where Jade knew Destinee would have problems reaching them. As Jade endured another lecture in front of customers about keeping the store set up according to the planogram, a face she hadn't seen in weeks waltzed through the door.

Russet dreadlocks, wide nose, a bright blue shirt... and a man on his arm.

Jade's heart pounded in her chest. Well, what did she expect? She never called him.

But that had only been three weeks ago, and it was obvious these men were in a relationship with the way they were hanging off each other.

He had flirted with her at a club when he was taken? How cruel could you get? The spot on the back of her hand that he'd kissed burned in shame.

"Are you even listening to me?"

Jade turned her glare on to her regional manager. "She's a lot faster when she can actually reach the pitchers. It's called reasonable accommodation. Not that being left-handed is a disability. But when you have a line out the door, certain things just make sense." She smirked, trying to hide it under a smile. "But then you'll figure that out on your own, won't you? When the store's numbers drop."

She pushed past Leanne's gaping maw to take over at the cash register so Miguel could take his break. And of course, she had to serve Andrew and his boyfriend.

Her customer service grin masked her pain. "Welcome to The Bean. What can I get y'all?"

"One chai mocha and a dragon fruit smoothie."

She rattled off their total and waited for him to swipe the card. Destinee was already making the drinks, but now she was on her tiptoes trying to pick up a pitcher. Jade reached over to grab one for her just as the entire pyramid started to fall.

When the pile of plastic crashed to the ground, the talking in the shop ceased. She glanced at Leanne out of the corner of her eye. Her boss had that 'I'm about to yell' look about her. Calmly, she handed Destinee the only pitcher in the cafe that was now clean so she could finish the order, and started pulling more off the floor.

"What are you *doing*?" Leanne hissed.

"We have to wash the pitchers, or else we can't make any more smoothies." Jade passed her three. "Let's go."

For once Leanne followed her to the back room, where there was a sink they used for washing dishes during the day.

"These are supposed to go into the dishwasher!"

"And at the end of the night, they do. Until then, we wash them by hand so that we can actually serve our customers."

"They have to go in there every time." Leanne said as she filled the top rack of the device.

"And we won't be able to make anything with the blender for two hours. That's sales suicide."

"It's policy."

Jade leaned against the sink. This was ridiculous. She had a new job, she had no intention of returning, or using this place as a reference ever again. Leanne would just have to learn that the corporate theories didn't work in practice the hard way.

But she hated leaving the kids in this wench's care. When she looked up, Destinee was at the door, sorrow in her eyes and a heavy set to her mouth.

Get out of here, she mouthed. *We'll be fine.*

Jade nodded. Then she wiped her hands on a paper towel and pulled her apron and visor off. "I wish you luck with the bullshit corporate thinks works, Leanne. I won't be dealing with irate customers who want an iced coffee for the next two hours."

"What?" Leanne's question was almost silenced by the hum of the dishwasher turning on.

"You're an idiot, and I'm done."

"You can't leave yet!"

"What are you going to do, fire me? It's my last day!" Jade grabbed her purse and flipped Leanne the bird as she exited the back door.

She was going to enjoy her freedom before her new job started on Monday.

Andrew poured himself some coffee into his Neon Unicorn mug, a birthday gift from his twin. Aiden had designed the logo. The image practically glowed against the black ceramic. He doctored it with creamer and sugar, then allowed the initial sip to hit him. The office manager was starting today. Thankfully, Mom was planning to show her around and get her settled into her role. He'd have to train her on certain software, but that could wait until tomorrow.

Let Monica ensure she didn't run away screaming on her first day.

Thinking about his mother apparently summoned her.

"This is the break room. You can put your lunch in the fridge up here. And there's coffee if you want."

Turning his head, Andrew's eyes bulged and his muscles clenched.

"Ah, Andrew, there you are. I'd like you to meet our new office manager…"

"Jade?" He finished for her. Mom cocked her head at Andrew, then looked back and forth between them. Ignoring the small smile on her face, he focused on the African goddess staring blankly at him in a gray skirt and pink blouse.

"I take it you know each other?"

"We've met." Jade's voice was ice cold, and she was clearly not pleased to see him.

"Well, Andrew is one of the owners I was telling you about."

He watched her prominent Adam's apple bob as she swallowed. Adam's apple? The lights in the club had hidden that little detail from him, and he sipped his coffee in amusement.

That was interesting.

"One of the owners?" Her voice came out subdued, and he hated it.

"Yes, the other is my brother."

Jade merely nodded her understanding.

Monica raised an eyebrow but said nothing, ignoring the tension. But he was sure she'd ask about it later. "Well, I'll show you to your desk, and we'll get your paperwork squared away."

Jade followed Mom from the room, and Andrew watched her hips sway as she left.

Why hadn't she messaged him? And why was she acting so cold?

He admonished himself for those thoughts as his legs carried him back to his office. She was an employee now, and even more off-limits than before. The last thing he needed was a sexual harassment scandal for the club when it was so new.

But the numbers didn't hold his focus like they normally did.

The next day she returned, this time in a plaid skirt and crisp white blouse. And Andrew had to torture himself by training her on the scheduling program. They sat huddled around her desk, her scent filling his nose, but her body language was rigid and uninterested. She apparently wanted to forget they'd met.

Jade watched his demonstration, and he let her take over. She didn't ask any questions and seemed to pick up the software flawlessly. Releasing the mouse was a mistake, because then all he could think about were those plump lips, now a glossy muted pink.

Andrew leaned back in his chair, clearly unneeded and unwanted. The dream he'd had of her the night before had left him hard and aching that morning, and he still had no idea what he had done wrong.

His mouth opened without his permission. "You never texted me."

Jade's hands stilled on the keyboard. "I had my reasons."

Her reasons? What the hell? "You knew you'd applied for the job. It's not a stretch to think that things could get awkward if you didn't."

"Things could get awkward if I *did* as well. Did you consider that?" Her soft voice had a sharp edge to it. But he was too frustrated to heed the warning.

"You could mention it. Instead of leaving me hanging for over a week."

"You certainly don't seem to lack for company."

Andrew drew back. "I come to work, I go home, and I visit my parents. That's it."

"And now you're a liar."

"What the hell are you talking about?"

"I saw you Sunday at the coffee shop I used to manage. You didn't recognize me then, but now you do? Come on. You just didn't want your boyfriend to know you handed out your number to a girl at the club."

Sunday? Boyfriend?

"I don't have a boyfriend."

"Well, that's not the vibe y'all gave off." She pushed away from the desk and stood. So did he. "I won't tell him, if that's what you're worried about. But he deserves better than that."

"I didn't even leave my apartment until dinner time on Sunday." He blinked. "How did you see me? I haven't laid eyes on you since that night you were out with your friends."

Jade shook her braids and started to walk away. "I'm going on break."

With that, Aiden bounded up the stairs with his usual golden retriever energy. "What's shakin', Bro?"

Andrew spoke through gritted teeth. "Aiden, meet our new office manager. Jade, this is the other owner of the club, my twin, Aiden Monroe."

Chapter 5

Jade wavered on her heels, heart racing like she'd spotted a ghost. "T-twin?"

"Great to have you on board! Say, I've seen you before..." Andrew's doppelgänger in loud clothing cocked his head at her. This was eerie. "Weren't you at The Bean on Sunday? My boyfriend Jeffrey loves their coffee."

Fuck. That hadn't been Andrew. It was Aiden!

Jade fell backwards into her chair, and Andrew leaned over, his forehead creased with concern.

"Are you okay?"

Her skull was a helium balloon, all floaty and shit. "Uh, I'm woozy..."

"How long ago did you eat?" Aiden asked.

Jade shook her head. "Didn't have time."

Andrew shot off. "I'll be right back."

Aiden stood guard. "You shouldn't miss breakfast sweetie, that's the most important meal of the day."

Unfortunately, the bus waited for no one. But she couldn't drum up the energy to explain that in order to get to the club by eight-thirty for her shift, she had to transfer buses and wake up just as early as she had for the coffee shop.

At least at The Bean, she could easily grab breakfast.

Andrew hurried over with her lunch bag. "Are you sure there's food in here? It doesn't weigh much."

Jade's eyes burned with embarrassment as she snatched her pack from him. It wasn't a lot, but it was what she could afford until she got paid. She hadn't realized how often she supplemented her meals with day-old pastries until she'd left the cafe.

She opened the bag and took out her sandwich, apple, and gelatin snack cup. Sure, it was only eleven, but the way she had nearly fainted at finding out Andrew had a twin was concerning.

"Dude, let her eat and come to my office for a second."

The man in question hesitated. "I'll be right back."

Alone at last, Jade bit into her ham-and-processed-cheese-food on wheat bread. She chewed slowly at first, the low blood sugar making her sluggish. But as she polished off the sandwich, she found it easier to eat her apple. And then her gelatin cup went down quickly.

All too soon, Andrew returned to her desk. He sat and smoothed his tie down, his cheeks flushed. What could Aiden have said to him to make him so flustered?

"Can—"

"Andrew, I—"

They spoke at the same time, then stopped and each waited for the other to speak. After a while, Andrew broke the silence.

"You go first."

A gentleman? Jade wished he wasn't, which was a new feeling for her. It only served to make her feel worse. "I owe you an apology, Andrew. I thought... well, I guess you know what I thought now." It was difficult to keep her gaze on his face. God, this was embarrassing. "I just never would have expected there was anyone out there who looked remotely like you."

One side of his lips curled up in a shadow of a smile. "That sounds like a compliment."

She had to change the subject, fast. "What were you going to say?"

Leaning back in his chair, he crossed his arms. She almost missed what he said with the way his biceps strained against the white cotton sleeves distracted her. "I was about to tell you I was taking you to lunch."

Butterflies erupted in her belly, and Jade's brain went, *"Excuse me?"*

But her mouth said, "I've already eaten, though."

He eyed the remains of her meal on the desk. "I suspect you'll be hungry again in an hour."

As if to prove him right, her stomach growled. "God damn it," she muttered under her breath, and unconsciously searched the room for a way out. But with so few people in the offices upstairs, she knew the only place to hide was the ladies' bathroom. And she couldn't stay in *there* all day!

Andrew let out a sigh. "If you're not comfortable going somewhere with me, I understand. I'll order in for us. But I'm worried you'll pass out if that's all you have to eat until five o'clock."

"I, um, okay." What was it about this guy that had her so flustered? And why was she disappointed that he was acting like a concerned boss rather than an interested date?

He leaned in. "DiAmato's down the street makes their own pasta from scratch. How's that sound?"

She nodded as she stared into a pair of stunning gray eyes. Taking a deep breath, she inhaled his cologne, which didn't help her nerves at all. Seconds ticked by, and neither moved.

Say something!

Jade licked her lips. "Ordering in sounds great."

"Alright." He pulled out his phone and clicked a few buttons. "Here's the menu."

She was really doing this. She was going to have lunch with her hot boss.

Jade made the first selection she saw, which was spaghetti and meatballs. Then she turned back to the computer. "Where do I post the schedule?"

The spell broken, Andrew showed her how to print it off, and then led her to the small copy room with the only printer for the entire building. On top of the laser printer was a sign that said "D.I.Y. Color Printer" and a box of crayons.

"What the hell?" He removed the art supplies from the unit and flipped up the monitor screen. "Aiden's too lazy to go down to the storage closet and get new ink?"

"Doesn't that fall under *my* duties?"

"I don't know. I didn't write your job description." Andrew bit out.

Jade drew back. What the fuck was his issue? He'd been giving her emotional whiplash all morning, and she had no idea what to expect. She'd apologized for her assumption he wasn't single, yet he still had an attitude problem.

"Maybe I should ask Monica."

He hung his head. "I am so sorry, Jade. I'm not mad at you; just frustrated with my brother. It's unfair of me to take it out on you."

"Well, it sounds like something an office manager should maintain. Why don't you show me where the storage room is?"

❧

Aiden's words in private rang in Andrew's mind.

"That's Jade? Is she your *Jade?"*

She wasn't his, not by a long shot. "The one I met at the club? Yes."

Aiden threw his head back and laughed. "Your face. Holy shit. You want her."

He tried to keep his voice down. "Doesn't matter. If she wanted to pursue something, she would have used the number I gave her."

Shit. He hadn't meant to spill that.

His twin's eyes bugged out. "You gave her your number? Why didn't you say so?"

Andrew pinched the bridge of his nose. "You never asked."

"So ask her out. Get to know her."

"Aiden! She's our employee now. I can't date her!"

His brother shook his head. "There's no rule that says that. Because we're in charge and we make the rules."

"It would be inappropriate."

Aiden crossed his arms. "Andrew, we run a nightclub for people society has deemed 'sexual deviants.' Inappropriate is our thing."

He fisted his locs. The desire to learn about her and the need to tow an invisible line he'd had in place for years vied for dominance.

Aiden clasped his shoulder. "Take her to lunch, as a work situation. Clearly the poor thing's starving. Get to know her as a coworker, and then see if it goes anywhere." He released

Andrew, then smirked. "Although it would be faster to press her up against the printer in the copy room and kiss the hell out of her."

"Aiden!" He hissed. But the images his brother's words inspired weren't unlike his dreams of late. Now he was thinking about bending her over the desk in his office, shimmying that pencil skirt she wore over her hips and bringing them both to climax...

Leading her downstairs to the storage area at the back of the club, he wrestled with even dirtier fantasies of stripping her naked in the dark closet that first night they met. He could have given her a birthday to remember.

Damn that asshole for starting a fight at the exit.

Jade followed him down the hallway to the tiny storage room, close enough that her heat pressed into him, though they didn't touch. Her citrus perfume, or body wash, he wasn't sure, surrounded him. Swallowing as he opened the painted black door, he pulled the string to turn on the light.

Shadows ran from the single bulb hanging from the ceiling. He pointed out various things she might need and grabbed one of the toner cartridges before turning around and stumbling into her.

"Sorry," they both said at the same time as he caught her elbow.

"It's not exactly big enough for two people in here." Sweat beaded on his forehead at her nearness. He stared up at her, not as far as the night they met. Those lips were in perfect kissing range. All he had to do was close the distance between them and...

Think unsexy thoughts. He started listing accounting rules in his head to keep himself in check.

Jade stepped out of his hold, her head down. She had been attracted to him that night. So why hadn't she texted? What was her "reason?"

"Thanks for showing me where this is."

"Sure," he answered. Then he kicked himself internally, remembering why pursuing this wasn't a good idea.

Get to know her as a coworker. That's all you can be.

"Delivery for Andrew?" rang out from the lobby. He squeezed past Jade, ignoring her intake of breath as their bodies touched.

After tipping the driver and taking the bag of food, he motioned for Jade to go ahead up the stairs. "I'll show you how to install this after we eat."

That was a mistake. Now he had to watch her tight ass wiggle in that pencil skirt all the way up.

Andrew held in his groan and knew this was going to feature in his dreams tonight.

Coworkers. Friends. Keep it together, man.

Aiden met them at the top of the stairs. "Ooh, what's for lunch?"

"Get your own, asshole."

"I do have my own asshole. Everyone does."

Now Andrew groaned out loud. "Can you not make crude jokes when we're in mixed company?"

"Lighten up, twin!" He elbowed Jade in the arm. "I have been reminding him this is a nightclub and not a bank. He spent way too many years in banking."

Jade gave Aiden an uncertain smile. Then a rumble came from her stomach again.

"Let me feed our office manager already."

"Oh fine. I'll just call Jeffrey and see if he wants to meet up." Then Aiden bounced down the stairs.

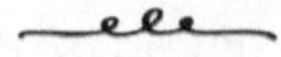

Jade was completely out of her depth. The brothers had such conflicting personalities; it was hard to find her footing. She'd been comfortable despite her misery at The Bean; she knew where she stood and what they expected of her.

Now she was in tight quarters with Mr. Hot Stuff from her birthday, and he was buying her lunch. While his mirror image made dirty jokes.

As your boss, Jade reminded herself. *This is not a date!*

She'd only asked Monica about a fraternization policy because Nadia insisted. Besides, she had been thinking Andrew worked security. That they'd be on an equal level.

The entire reason Ben, her favorite regional manager ever, had left The Bean was because of his relationship with one of his store managers. Other stores filed complaints he was giving his girlfriend's cafe special treatment, and instead of letting corporate draw it out and demote or fire him, he high-tailed it to another company.

So the thought of dating a boss made her anxious. No way in hell would she do anything to jeopardize this job.

Jade and Andrew ate without speaking for several minutes. The pasta was out of this world with thick, chewy noodles in a bright tomato sauce and three huge meatballs.

He finally broke their stalemate as the silence stretched into awkward territory. "What do you do in your free time, Jade?"

"Hang out with my friends, read." No need to tell the hot guy about their *Dungeons and Dragons* campaign.

"What do you read?"

She squirmed in her chair. "Comics," she reluctantly answered. Yep, now her sexy boss would move on, and they could keep things from getting uncomfortable at the office.

When he leaned forward, interest sparking in his gray eyes, she realized her mistake. "Did you say comics?"

Shit. Jade hadn't taken him for a nerd. She shoved half a meatball in her mouth to make sure she didn't tell him anything else and nodded.

"DC or Marvel?"

She stirred her pasta some more and chewed slowly. Please let him be a DC fan. They'd never get along.

"Marvel, but I haven't been keeping up with them." Money for comics had been nonexistent since she moved out of the dorms.

"Which series?"

"I grew up reading X-Men."

The grin that spread across his face could light up the building. And it revealed dimples. Damn, that was so unfair.

"They're my favorite, too."

And they were back to being awkward again. Jade said the first thing that came to mind. "This food is amazing. Thanks for lunch."

"You're welcome."

The day went much smoother after that. They settled into a sort of professional truce. But restraining her desire was exhausting. And she needed to talk to her squad.

Jade: Anyone wanna hang out tonight?

Rosie: I have to do laundry.

Mia: I'm free!

Nadia: I can swing by for a little bit.

Olivia: Kinda regret moving out now.

Jade: You have wheels.

Olivia: True. And work in the morning.

Nadia: It is convenient to get together in our pajamas.

Rosie: What's up, Jade? How's the new job?

Jade: That's what I want to talk to y'all about.

Rosie: Why doesn't everyone come here? I'll just have to jump down to the basement every so often.

Jade: Fine by me.

It took Jade two hours to make it home by bus, but the wait was worth it. By the time she got there, Nadia had cooked dinner for everybody and Rosie had thrown cookies in the oven. Mia brought a salad. Olivia showed up with a bottle of wine. Damn, she missed this.

The entire scene made her nostalgic for the days when they shared an on-campus apartment in college. It was rare that they all had free time at once anymore.

They sat around Rosie's table, dishing out food and pouring alcohol. "So how's the new job working out?" asked Olivia.

Jade swallowed her bite of salad and laid her fork down. "Everyone put their beverages down; I don't want y'all to choke." The squad looked at each other, then back at her as they set their glasses down. "You remember Hot Stuff from my birthday?"

"Oh yeah, he was fiiiiine." Mia waggled her eyebrows.

"Well, I told y'all he said he worked there."

"Yeah, we remember," replied Rosie. "So, you work together now?"

"Sort of." Jade pursed her lips. "He's my *boss*."

"No way!" Mouths gaped and eyes bulged as her friends heard the news.

"Yep! He is one of the owners."

"Who are the others?" Mia asked.

"His mom and his *twin brother*."

Mia groaned. "Okay, that is *not* fair to have that much hotness in one family."

"Tell me about it!" Jade pretended to fan herself. "Although his brother has a boyfriend. They went to The Bean on my last day and I mistook him for Andrew.

Thought that he'd played me. So I was glad I didn't text him.

"Imagine my surprise when he's all, 'You never texted me' so I told him, 'I saw you with your boyfriend!' And then his doppelgänger comes up the stairs."

Olivia's blue eyes nearly popped out of her head. "You thought it was him, but it was his twin?"

"Yeah. That was *awkward as hell*." She took a sip of her wine.

Nadia shook her head. "Honey, I think you might need something stronger."

"Thanks, Nad, but I have to wake up at stupid o'clock to get there on the bus, so I'll pass. This weekend though—you're on."

"You got it, friend." Nadia clinked her glass with Jade's and they both drank. "So, what about that fraternization policy?"

Jade sighed. "They don't have one, which makes sense cause they're so new and small, but this is my *boss* we're talking about. Not a security guy like I thought he was."

Olivia shrugged. "Hey, if there's no rule..."

"But that could get much more awkward! Plus, I work with his *mom*."

"I wouldn't worry about that if she's part owner as well. It's a gay club. She must be super chill with all of it." Mia took a bite of her chicken.

Jade sighed. "I'm not even sure if he'd be interested in me once he knew what I am. For all I know, he's simply supporting his brother." She pushed her food around on her plate. "It doesn't matter, though. I waited for a better job for so long, and I refuse to do anything to fuck it up."

Rosie laid a hand on her shoulder. "I get it. We just want to see you happy."

Warmth spread through her chest as Jade wrapped an arm around her friend. "I've got you four. What more could I need?" She blinked back the unexpected tears and squeezed tighter.

Chapter 6

IN THE BREAK ROOM above The Neon Unicorn, Aiden was telling the story of how he'd met his current beau. "When I finally met Jeff face to face, I swear my heart skipped a beat."

"That's arrhythmia and you should probably get that checked out," Jade said. Andrew was impressed with how she was able to keep a straight face. "Trust me, one of my best friends is a nurse."

"No! It was true love!"

"Sugar, don't make me start quoting *The Princess Bride*."

Andrew snickered as he carried his lunch bag to his office. Jade's gaze met his briefly over Aiden's head, then darted to the floor.

He'd fallen into a rhythm over the last few weeks. He carefully avoided being in the same room as Jade for too long, but made sure he still spoke to her throughout the day. It was a delicate, draining tightrope act.

Fighting this attraction wasn't easy, especially because not only was she beautiful, but smart and witty, too. At least she showed her sense of humor with his brother. Aiden had always been the fun twin, and Andrew often caught himself watching them from the door of his office, longing for her smile to be aimed at him.

He hadn't always been so reserved. But that was a younger Andrew, without the burdens of a business owner.

So all day he watched the one he would not let himself have, and then went home and worked his frustrations out at the gym every night. On nights he was lucky, he wore himself out and slept without dreaming of her.

The Thursday before Labor Day, when they were expecting a huge crowd thanks to the long weekend, he got a text in the middle of the afternoon.

Ember: Hey, I can't make it in tonight.

Andrew: No problem, I'll have Jade call the temp in. Are you okay? Can I drop something off for you?

Ember: Actually, could you pick me up and take me home? I'm finally getting discharged from the hospital.

Andrew: What the hell! What happened?

Ember: If you come get me, I'll explain on the way.

Andrew pulled up to the patient pickup area, and his stomach dropped to the floor when he saw his best friend. Ember's face was blue and black, her arm in a sling. Her braid was disheveled, and she looked utterly wrecked.

He pushed the passenger side door of his Explorer open. "What the fuck happened? And where's the body?"

She scoffed. "He got away. The cops didn't give me much hope. They think it was a one-off attack."

He helped her buckle her seatbelt when it became an obvious struggle for her. "Tell me everything."

Ember sighed and leaned back against the seat. "My car's in the shop, so I was waiting for the bus after work last night. Some asshole came up to me and yanked my hair, then started punching me in the face. Like, what did I ever do to him? I'd never met the guy! I fought hard, and I think I gave him a bloody nose, but he tried to throw me and twisted my arm. It injured my rotator cuff, and that hurts like a bitch, let me tell you." She shook a bottle of pills at him. "I have to take painkillers, so I can't even pick up my car when it's done tomorrow."

"Jesus Christ. Did he say anything to you?"

"Yeah, and that's what worries me the most." Ember leaned in and dropped her voice. "He called me a faggot tranny."

Andrew hissed in a breath. He was increasing security the minute he got back to the office. Hell, he'd call Aiden from Ember's apartment.

"That's terrifying."

"I know! And he's still out there. What if he attacks patrons next?"

"And the cops aren't doing anything?"

Ember rolled her eyes. "They registered my complaint, took the tissue samples from under my fingernails, but all they can do is patrol the area. And our customers will not like that much better."

"I'll tell Aiden to hire more people. We need to protect the customers." They'd find the money. His attention pulled to Ember's arm. "How long are you out for?"

"Two weeks. I'm so sorry. I know we just got that temp hired."

"You have nothing to apologize for. So we find another one."

Ember shook her head. "It's the worst time to be down a person."

"Let me handle it. Focus on getting better. And one of us will get your car when the mechanic is done."

She refused his offer of help to get into her apartment. Several times. After dropping her off and making sure she got inside, Andrew called his twin on the Bluetooth in his Explorer.

"Hey, Bro! I was just wondering — why aren't you at your desk?"

"Ember texted me. She needed a ride from the hospital."

"*What*?"

Andrew sighed, then relayed Ember's story to Aiden. His brother went silent, but not for long. "I'll contact the other businesses on that block, see if they have any cameras."

"Good idea, and I think we should hire extra security until he's caught."

He could hear the wheels in Aiden's mind turning on the other end of the phone. "Let's keep this quiet. I don't want to scare the patrons. But I can tell the guys to patrol outside."

"We should look into getting a camera installed on that corner, too." Andrew laid his forehead against his hand while he waited at the red light. Why hadn't they put one there to begin with?

"Good thinking. I can call the security company. And if anyone says they're waiting for the bus, I'll have the guys follow them for safety."

"Will you let Jade know Ember's going to be out for two weeks?"

Aiden let out a breath. "Ouch, that sucks. Yeah, I can tell her."

The light turned green, and Andrew was on his way back. "Ask Mom if she had any other temps that interviewed well. See if they're interested in a short-term assignment."

"Will do."

While he drove, he couldn't stop the memories of another assault victim from coming to mind, their face bruised and battered. That last conversation had decimated him, and he hadn't seen his high school sweetheart since he had run from their hospital room.

"I needed you! Where were you?"

Nearly twenty years later, and he still felt the pain of his teenage heartbreak. He wasn't present to stop that fight, and he hadn't been available to protect Ember last night, either. But he would be damned if anyone else got hurt on his watch.

Jade sent another schedule to the printer with a sigh and a click of her mouse. She'd spent hours going back and forth on the phone with the bartenders to work out how to make Ember's time off happen. The new temp Monica was calling in helped, but their availability wasn't the same.

Casual Friday was her favorite thing about working in an office. She'd worn comfy sandals and her denim capris, and her favorite sleeveless shirt with Storm from the *X-Men* comic on it. Not to be confused with Halle Berry.

Andrew never dressed casually. He wore a polo and his dress pants. She wondered if the man even *owned* jeans.

The squad had come together with Marcia's Casa de Tatuajes crew for an early Labor Day picnic. She was due at Druid Hill Park after work. Unfortunately, the bus routes didn't run straight there, and it looked like she'd be lucky to get there before dark. At least she would have a little time with her friends.

Jade could call one of them and ask for a ride. But that would require them to leave the party right amid setting up. And the Unicorn was far away from everything...

Hopefully, she could save up enough to buy a car soon.

She left her itinerary up on her screen as she strode to the printer, grabbed the new schedule, then headed for the stairs to post it for the other employees downstairs. But she stopped as she passed her desk. Andrew was standing behind it, staring at her computer.

"Can I help you with something?" They'd been friendlier since that first day, but for him to invade her personal space like this brought her right back to the same level of rage as when she'd thought he had a boyfriend.

"You take the bus?"

"Yeah, that's what most people without cars do."

"Jade... you can't."

Excuse me? "I'm a grown woman and I most certainly can!"

He pointed at the screen, which held her itinerary. "Two hours to go to a park only twenty minutes from here? Ridiculous!"

"That's public transportation, sugar." She waltzed down the stairs to hang up the schedule, shaking her head at his privilege. When she got back, he was still there. Except now, he sat behind her desk in her chair.

"Why are you in my seat?"

"I can drive you."

Jade huffed a breath. "I don't need you to take me to a picnic with my friends, Andrew. I've taken the bus every day for years."

"Not from here, you haven't."

It was Friday, and the first long weekend that she would *actually* be able to enjoy since high school. The clock was ticking down the minutes to five o'clock and she had to get out of there right on schedule to catch that bus.

And her hot boss was giving her a migraine. "What is your *deal*?"

Andrew looked away, and his voice dropped to a whisper. "That's where Ember was attacked." He glanced back at her, but only for a moment. "The police won't have caught the guy yet, and we haven't had time to increase security or install a camera on that corner. We haven't said anything because we didn't want to scare anyone. But I had no idea any of the employees took the bus regularly. Ember usually drives, but her car was in the shop." His gray eyes pleaded for her forgiveness. "If I'd known, I would have told you."

Jade tried to ignore the way her heart melted. "Fine. I'll let you drive me tonight. And just so you won't worry, my friends are counting on giving me a ride home. We all live in the same building."

He nodded, but said nothing. "Let me shut down my computer and get ready to go."

Andrew's cologne assailed her senses as he brushed past her and she had to lean against the wall to avoid swooning. She finished her work and closed up her machine on auto-pilot, kicking herself for agreeing to be in a confined space with him for a full twenty minutes. How was she going to hide her attraction?

At least once she arrived at the park, she would be free.

Jade was right; the drive was torture. His fingers brushed hers when he put the car into gear, and his woodsy scent was *everywhere*. It was embedded in this SUV. And he had the air conditioning on so she couldn't be rude and open a window.

She wanted to bathe in that smell, but she didn't dare.

Andrew found the pavilion her friends had rented out easily, pulling into a parking space between Jake's SUV and Rosie's sedan.

"Thanks for the ride." Jade started to exit the vehicle.

"Hang on a minute," Andrew left his Explorer and circled around. When he held open the door for her, her pulse pounded in her ears.

"You don't need to do this. We're not on a date."

"My mom would have my head if I didn't. Please." He extended a hand to her, and she took it, sliding her feet to the pavement.

She nearly jumped when Andrew followed her up to the park. "What are you doing?"

"I'm going to use the public facilities before I go home. Why?"

She looked him up and down. "I just figured you'd let me out at the curb and that would be that."

"Number one, Monica raised a gentleman. Number two, I have to piss."

Jade laughed. "I'll see you Tuesday."

Just then, Matt called out. "Hey Jade! Burgers are almost done... Andrew? What are you doing here?"

Andrew lifted his eyebrows when he looked at her. "How do you know Matt?"

She straightened her spine. "I've known his sister Olivia since we were both in college. Plus, he's living with my friend Rosie." Rosie wasn't far from her man, who was tending the grill with Eddie, Marcia's cousin. "Where did you meet him?"

He shrugged. "We were at a conference together last year. He was there as part of a class; I was just there to learn about liquor licenses."

Matt waved them over, and Rosie walked up and hugged Jade. "Come on, drinks are over there in the cooler."

"Sounds good to me." There better be something strong enough in there for her to get through this.

⁓ eee ⁓

Andrew shook Matt's hand, shocked to see the kid here. When he last saw him, Matt hadn't grown his blonde beard in fully yet, but it was nice and even now. It made him look older than his twenty-two years.

"You graduated this year, right?"

"Yup." Matt turned back to his cooking partner. "You good, Eddie?"

"Yeah, man, I can lift the food. You round everyone up."

"I can take care of that," a short, curvy brunette said. "Hi, I'm Rosie, one of Jade's friends. And Matt's girlfriend."

"Nice to meet you, Rosie." Andrew shook her hand as she left the patio where the grill was situated.

"I thought you lived in Virginia."

Matt pulled his apron off over his head. "I did. But I got an internship at the Orange Blossom and took over my sister's lease. Then they hired me on."

"Congratulations!" The Orange Blossom was a high-end restaurant. While Andrew hadn't been there, he had certainly heard of it.

"Thanks. How did your club opening go?"

"We're still smoothing some things out, but business is good."

"Great to hear. Say, why don't you join us? There's plenty of food."

Andrew saw Jade give Matt a death glare behind him, but he didn't want to be rude. And it smelled fantastic.

"I'd be honored. Do you know where the bathroom is, by any chance?"

Matt pointed out a cinderblock building, then handed him a bottle of hand sanitizer. "The park hasn't restocked the soap, apparently."

"Got it. I'll be right back."

When he returned with the sanitizer, everyone was loading their plates buffet-style off a picnic table laden with food. There was so much packed on there, people had brought camping chairs just to sit and eat. Others were standing around. Matt handed him a plate and thankfully, stuck by him. A group of girls surrounded Jade, and she didn't seem interested in talking to him.

"So how do you know Jade? She never brings dates to these things."

Andrew almost choked on his hot dog. "Date? No no no, she works for me at the club. I was honestly just stopping to use the restroom when you saw us."

"*That's* where Jade's new job is. I remember Rosie mentioned it, but it didn't click that it was your club."

"Yeah, we needed an office manager. I offered to drive her here because there was no direct bus route." Okay, that wasn't the *real* reason he'd driven her, but he really did not want to go into their additional security problem at a party and kill the mood.

"Well, it's good to see you again. Now that I'm living in Baltimore, we should get drinks sometime."

"Sounds good. I'll give you my number before I go."

Matt swallowed the last of his burger. "Are you taking her home, too?"

"I would, but she said her friends were counting on driving her." Since his protective streak had flared, he found himself curious as to Jade's security. Although given her work history, he doubted she lived anywhere with a door-man or a camera.

Or maybe he just wanted to torture himself some more in her presence.

Matt cleared his throat and spoke low, so only Andrew heard. "Are you sure this isn't a date?"

Andrew matched his blue gaze. "Positive."

He gave Andrew a knowing look. "You've barely taken your eyes off her the whole time we've talked."

Andrew felt his cheeks darken, and Matt chuckled. Damn his fair coloring. "We initially met when she was out dancing with her friends at the Unicorn."

"Interesting."

"Matt, I'm her boss. You know how rife our industry is with sexual harassment cases." Everyone had heard about that celebrity television chef who had fallen from grace that way a few years back. The negative publicity decimated his career.

"It's only harassment if it's not wanted. Might be worth feeling her out."

Andrew shook his head. "My brother and I worked too hard to start this business." The Neon Unicorn had been their dream for years.

"Talk to her. Don't get me wrong, Jade's scary as fuck when she wants to be. But if my own relationship has taught me anything, it's that you should *never* assume you know what they want." Matt polished off his potato salad and headed for the cooler. "Discuss it like adults. Then if she says she's not interested, just back off. You'll be fine."

Andrew accepted his offer to get him another soda, then returned to watching Jade interact with her friends. They were laughing about a joke he was too far away to catch, and he smiled despite himself. Her radiance shone like a beacon, and his heart tugged with the force of a puppy on a leash.

He didn't want to ignore this any longer.

Chapter 7

JADE FOUGHT THE URGE to look back at Andrew. "He's my boss, and he insisted on driving me over. I didn't realize he knew Matt."

"So why hasn't he taken his eyes off you since you got here?" Nadia's amused green gaze didn't miss a thing. Jade feigned nonchalance and shrugged.

"How the fuck should I know?"

Olivia leaned in close. "Don't tell Jake I said this, but he's hot as hell, Jade. If there's no policy against it..."

She shook her head. "I am not going there. He hasn't exactly been friendly. And he bulldozed me into letting him drive me here." She might be able to handle an alpha male, but it grated on her nerves.

Just because she presented as a woman did not mean she was weak.

"You said he has a twin, right?" Luckily, Rosie diverted the group's attention. "What's he like?"

"Aiden is much more approachable. They look the same, but they act so differently. It's a bit of a mind fuck. I don't know how I didn't realize he wasn't Andrew at The Bean."

"And he's just as hot, right?" Mia snickered as Marcia smacked her arm with the back of her hand. But there was no heat behind it. Mia just liked to be nosy.

"Sure, if you're into gay men." Jade chuckled. Aiden was no more attracted to her than a broom. "Plus, he has a boyfriend."

"Oh, right. Well, there went that idea." Mia relaxed in her seat and grabbed her girlfriend's palm so she couldn't pretend to hit her again. "How's the job otherwise? We never hear from you in the group chat."

Jade wiped her mouth on her napkin. "It's great. I mean, it sucks one of our bartenders is out for two weeks. Doing the schedule today gave me a headache. But other than that, everything is fine. I love not being on my feet eight hours a day." Although the commute was a hassle. "I'm just so tired from the bus ride when I get home. I don't have time for much more than eating and falling into bed."

Olivia polished off her hard lemonade. "You'll be car shopping before you know it. And then it won't be so bad."

She hoped so.

The rest of the evening passed pleasantly, surrounded by her squad. The guys returned to their shirts versus skins football game while the girls chatted with Annie, a tattoo artist at Eddie's shop, and her companion Jinx. Annie glowed with her pregnancy, but it was also the reason the two of them left first. Jinx was an excellent partner; Jade could see them holding back the urge to hover. Yet the relief on their face when an exhausted Annie suggested they leave was palpable.

Her gaze kept following Andrew without her permission as the football flew into his arms. His dreads flowed behind him as he ran and dodged Javier, who was playing on the skins side. This new view of him intrigued her; messy, sweaty, and whooping as he spiked the ball in a touchdown. Maybe her uptight boss *could* cut loose once in a while.

That didn't excuse his thinking she couldn't take the damn bus in broad daylight.

Before she realized it, the streetlights blinked on one by one and the cicadas began their nighttime chirping. "Nad, can you give me a ride home?" Jade had been having such a good time with her friends she hadn't noticed it getting dark out. Cars filled up fast as people made their way out of the park. She joined her squad as they all rushed to clean up what was left.

"Sorry, Jade. I'm spending the night at Caleb's."

"Mia?"

"*Ay bendito,* we have to drive my cousin and some of my crew home first. Her car's full." Marcia looked contrite.

Mia giggled. "I can't wait to see Eddie's face when he has to get inside the 'Barbie Clown Car.'" She even added little drunken air quotes around it as she staggered alongside her girlfriend.

Jade turned to Rosie, who was apologetic as she gathered paper plates and trash. "I guess the Casa Crew is all too drunk to drive. We're driving the rest of them home."

Shit. She hadn't planned on riding the bus back from the park. She'd been counting on one of the girls to come through to help her. Matt whispered in Rosie's ear as Olivia tapped Jade on the shoulder.

"We can drop you off on our drive home."

"I'll take you." Andrew sauntered over. Or he looked like he sauntered. It was getting hard to see, since the picnic area didn't have many lights.

"It's out of the way for both of you." Jade sighed.

Andrew crossed his arms. "But I haven't had anything to drink, and Jake looks like he's going to fall asleep."

He had abstained? Had he planned this?

"Olivia used to live in my building. She knows where it is."

Just then, Jake walked over with the now-empty beverage container. "Princess, how did we get everything into the trunk? I can't fit the cooler in." His voice was exhausted, and Jade remembered he was only a peewee coach, and hadn't played football that hard in years.

She swallowed her pride, watching Olivia rush forward to help carry his burden. He looked like he might drop it. They needed to get home as soon as possible. She turned back to Andrew, who had come right up next to her.

A tiny intake of breath betrayed her surprise at finding him so close. In her flat shoes, they were eye-to-eye. Her heart beat faster at the thought of riding in an enclosed space with him again. Somehow, his scent was even stronger since the football game.

"I don't want to put you out. You already came out of your way to bring me here."

"It's no trouble." His gaze softened as it dropped to her lips, causing her to look at his. He darted his tongue out to wet them, and she glanced away.

This was a mistake. But she couldn't ask Olivia and Jake to take her home when Andrew was clear-headed and not tired in the least. Was that because he was a nightclub owner?

It hit her how exhausted she was, and she decided one more trip in her boss's car wouldn't kill her. "Okay."

After Jade said goodbye to her friends, Andrew led her over to his Explorer. Humidity hung thick in the air, the moon shrouded behind clouds. At least the parking lot was well lit. He walked ahead so he could open her door for her. Based on the look she gave him, Jade wasn't used to guys doing that for her.

It gave him a tiny thrill.

He turned the engine over and they both breathed in the cool air-conditioning after sitting outside for the last several hours. It was Jade that broke the silence first.

"Did you have a good time?"

"Yeah. Your friends are great." He'd had far more fun than he thought he would. Another awkward pause. Then Andrew realized he didn't know where he was going.

He brought the navigation system up on his built-in console. "What's your address?"

She rattled it off, and the computer calculated his route. Just as they were leaving the park, the skies opened up and dumped one last summer storm.

"Lovely." Jade's voice dripped with sarcasm.

Andrew smirked and spoke without thinking. "This would have been a lousy night to wait for the bus."

She was quiet for several moments, and he grew terrified he'd offended her. Damn it, he needed to do better. "Thank you," she whispered at last.

He pondered her response. "Happy to do it. I try to take care of my… people." Andrew knew he couldn't call her his friend, not yet. So "people" would have to do.

Another few beats of silence. "You treat all employees this way?"

Shit, she had him cornered. "Well, I'm not close to everyone. I've known Ember for years, we were best friends in college. So she called me to get a ride from the hospital."

Jade hummed in her throat. "And she's the reason you don't want me taking the bus."

Andrew squirmed in his seat. He didn't want to scare her, but he needed her to understand why. "I saw what he did to her, Jade. Her arm's in a sling. He injured her rotator cuff, and beat her up." An image of Jade's face with Ember's injuries superimposed over it flashed across his mind, and he shivered. "You're at a higher risk than anyone else."

"How so?"

Stopped at the red light that led to her street, Andrew contemplated whether he should tell Jade what the assailant had said. And when he thought about it, he realized Ember would smack him for not telling Jade a lot sooner.

He couldn't let her get hurt.

"Ember said her attacker called her a tranny." Jade hissed in a breath. "He's targeting trans women, sweetheart. *That's* why I flipped."

Andrew pulled into a space in front of a pharmacy whose neon light blinked, showing they were still open. Jade's silence filled his car.

When she finally spoke, her voice trembled. "How long have you known I'm trans?"

That was an odd thing to ask. He turned to face her and met her fearful, wide-eyed gaze. "Since your first day on the job."

She furrowed her eyebrows. "Really?"

"Yeah."

"You didn't say anything."

He shrugged. "It's none of my business."

"But you gave me your number at the club…"

Andrew offered her a gentle smile. "It makes no difference to me, baby. I'm pansexual."

Her mouth dropped open and closed with an "Oh."

The rain wasn't letting up any time soon. Andrew reached behind them and fished an umbrella out from his backseat. "Here," he said, handing it to her. "You can return it to me on Tuesday."

She turned it over in her hands. "Thanks again."

He drank in the way the light reflected off her dark skin, her plush lips now devoid of lipstick, and those long lashes. It would have to last him three days. "Good night."

"Night, Andrew."

She raced away under the deluge, slipping inside a door and disappearing from view. Then he drove himself home.

By the time he got there, it was late, and the storm showed no signs of letting up. Shaking the water from his hair, he slipped his shoes off and left them to make a puddle on the welcome mat. Silence echoed around his space. It reverberated straight into his heart, inciting a deep longing. As he stripped and headed for the shower, Andrew had to face the truth.

He was sick of coming home to an empty apartment. And the only person he wanted to fill the void was his employee.

Two days later, that thought still plagued his mind. Which made Sunday dinner at his parents' house uncomfortable as hell. Jeffrey had become a regular attendee, which thrilled Monica and Stuart Monroe to no end. This week, it only emphasized to Andrew that he had never brought anyone home.

Jesus Christ. He was thirty-five years old and hadn't had an adult relationship worthy of meeting the family.

While he contemplated his failures, his twin carried the conversation. That wasn't all that unusual. But something must have shown on his face, because Dad pulled him into their garish red rooster-themed kitchen to wash dishes.

"What have you been brooding about all night?" If Monica Monroe was a force of nature, Stuart Monroe was gravity. Inevitable.

"I have not been brooding. I just have a lot on my mind."

Dad raised one salt-and-pepper eyebrow at him. "You've barely said a word all evening and these are clearly not happy thoughts."

He sighed as laughter pierced the air, driving home his point. "I miss that."

"You miss dating?"

Not in so many words. Dating as an adult was rough. "I miss having someone special."

His dad started rinsing plates and handing them to him to place in the dishwasher. Since his retirement, Stuart had softened, his stomach more rounded, but as always, he made sure to pull his weight around the house. It was a quality he'd been certain to instill in his sons. "Your mom mentioned something about your new office manager."

Andrew's cheeks heated, and he knew his father noticed.

Dad's teeth gleamed against his dark brown skin. "Want to tell me what that's all about?"

He groaned, but told his dad about how they'd first met when Andrew took Aiden's night shift at the club.

"Would it be so bad to date her?"

He scrubbed his hands down his face. "That could make things super awkward around the office if we don't work out. Or if the other employees feel she's getting special treatment." And then came the kicker. "There's no rule against it, but it feels forbidden."

Dad leaned back against the counter and crossed his arms. "I think I might know a thing or two about forbidden relationships." He wrapped an arm around Mom as she rounded the island and kissed his cheek.

"Your grandfather refused to give me away at our wedding."

Andrew hadn't heard this story before. Mom and Dad had always been tight-lipped about their nuptials. There were only a few photos of the two of them from that day. And while there was a forbidden aspect to interracial dating in his parents' time, that wasn't his situation. "It's not quite the same. I'm in a position of authority over her."

"True, but there's no rule against it." Monica winked at him.

Dad snorted. "Doesn't mean people won't tell you how to live your life."

"I'd rather he date her so we can go back to normal." Aiden wandered in with Jeffrey bringing up the rear. "You could cut the tension with a knife around those two."

"Aiden, we talked about this." Andrew sighed.

Mom raised her head from Dad's shoulder. "I'll change her position, so she reports to me. Would that help?"

"Maybe." He ran a hand over his dreadlocks. "You don't think it's a bad idea?"

"Pining after her all day isn't productive, either." A soft smile graced his mother's face. "It's not the bank, sweetheart. I doubt it will hurt anything."

Aiden elbowed him in the ribs. "Just promise you won't play around with this one. I like her and we can't afford to lose her." His twin became thoughtful. "She's a settle-down type of woman. And Mr. Serious hasn't had a relationship in a long time."

Andrew rolled his eyes. "You're a fine one to talk."

"Except I haven't been beating myself up over my high school sweetheart for the last twenty years."

He covered his face with his hand. "*Don't* bring them up."

"Andrew," his mom gasped as she laid her hands on his shoulders. "That wasn't your fault."

"What if I can't protect her?" He lowered his palm and glared at Aiden. Why did he have to remind him of his ex?

"You're older and wiser now." Aiden's serious expression disappeared as a teasing smirk returned. "And maybe you're already making your move. Word at the Unicorn is you drove Miss Aguillard home Friday evening, Brother." He wagged his eyebrows. "Methinks he doth protest too much."

Andrew gripped the back of his neck and glanced away. "She was going to ride the bus for two hours to go to a picnic that it only took me twenty minutes to drive her to. That's all."

Just like that, Aiden was on high alert. "Jade rides the bus?"

Jeffrey looked at them, confused. "What's wrong with that, babe?"

"Right now? Everything." Between the two of them, they caught his family up on what had happened to Ember, including the fact the attacker was trying to target trans women.

"That's awful!" Monica held her hand over her heart. "I hope the police catch him."

Aiden reached inside the refrigerator for a beer. "We're not just relying on the cops, Mom. I've got a crew setting up a camera on that corner first thing Tuesday, and I beefed up security. They know to patrol around the building now, so the team hopes if he strikes again, we'll get him before he hurts anyone else."

"What did the other businesses on that intersection say when you asked about recordings?" Andrew had hoped someone had been thinking further ahead than they had been. And he was still kicking himself for what had happened to Ember.

"They have cameras but not trained on the bus stop. The dog daycare and the barbershop were both going to go through their footage for the night of the attack and get back to me if they saw anything. And I gave their information to the police."

Andrew pulled his own beer from the refrigerator while his brother continued to discuss the plans to thwart Ember's assailant. While his concerns about Jade were again at the front of his mind, the realization that both his business partners had given their blessing to pursue something with her comforted him.

Now he just needed to ask her out.

<h1 style="text-align:center">Chapter 8</h1>

Jade shuffled into work Tuesday morning like a zombie. She'd barely slept all weekend, and going grocery shopping with the rest of Baltimore on a Saturday had been chaos. To make matters worse, Memaw had missed their weekly phone date — *again*. There'd been no answer at the old house and her grandmother didn't exactly believe in cell phones.

She had sounded weak and tired on the call three weeks ago, completely unlike herself. And Memaw wouldn't give her any details or talk about what was going on in her life. Jade may not be a Voodoo practitioner, but her instincts knew something was wrong.

Fuck the car. She had to save money to go to Louisiana.

So it was no wonder that she was passing out the mail that morning with an extra strong cup of coffee in one hand. Most of the envelopes went to Andrew. Her heart pounded as she slipped through his office door and saw him sitting behind his desk for the first time since Friday night.

He knew she was trans. And he hadn't run away yet, or rescinded his attraction. And he was definitely still attracted to her, if the heated look in his eyes at this moment was anything to judge by. He looked at her like she was a bottle of water in a desert.

Her distraction was her downfall. Literally.

A few feet from his desk, her shoe caught on the carpet and pitched her forward. Time slowed to a standstill as her beverage launched out of her cup, landing right on Andrew's face.

All she could think about as her chin hit the floor was, *Is he hurt?*

"Jade!"

Crap. She'd fucked it all up now. The first unicorn of mutual attraction she came across, and she'd thrown coffee at his head.

"Are you alright?" He squatted down in front of her.

"Are *you* okay?" She parroted back to him despite her teeth rattling around in her head and scrambled to her knees.

"I'm more worried about you."

"I burned you!"

"It wasn't that hot anymore."

They fussed at each other as Andrew lifted her by the elbows to her feet. Coffee drenched his shirt.

"Shit! And you have that supplier meeting today. I am *so* sorry. Let me run to the bathroom and get some paper towels."

"Jade. Jade!" He grabbed her shoulders and looked deep into her eyes. She hadn't been this close to him before. Those steel-gray orbs had green flecks, and she found herself mesmerized.

Then he breathed a sigh of relief, and his mouth curled up at one end. "Well, I don't think you have a concussion."

"My head doesn't hurt, just my teeth. And my pride." She kicked her heels off and decided to switch into the flats she carried for the bus. "Obviously, I'm not steady enough today to wear these. I'll change." His hands still gripped her upper arms. "It's okay, Andrew," she mumbled. "You can let go."

He licked those thick lips and his Adam's apple bobbed as he swallowed. "What if I don't want to?"

Maybe she *had* hit her head. "Huh?"

He released his fingers, but his hands stayed on her as they slid up her shoulders. Jade could taste cinnamon on his breath. That gray gaze searched hers, and Jade stared at his freckles as the moment dragged on, the only sound in the room the ticking of the ancient wall clock. Taking a deep breath, he muttered "Fuck it." Then he cupped her face and leaned in, pausing just as their noses grazed each other.

Jade's mouth dried up and her breathing became shallow. Her gaze locked on where his mouth hovered a breath away. *Do it,* she thought to herself, licking her lips. *Kiss me, already!*

Her shoes fell to the floor with a thud as his coffee-drenched lips finally made contact, caressing hers in a sensual dance. Jade's arms wrapped around his waist and she opened her mouth on a soft moan. The tip of his tongue toyed with hers, then slid home, making butterflies samba in her stomach. Good *Lord,* the man could kiss.

Jade didn't know how long it went on, but Andrew ended the best kiss of her life way too soon. Slowly, he drew back, then pressed his forehead against hers. Both of them were panting. Holy shit.

"Don't worry about the coffee."

"Coffee?" Jade's eyes blinked open to see his grin.

"I keep an extra shirt in the office."

Suddenly, she remembered what had led to him kissing her. "Oh, thank God."

He was already pulling his tie off and heading for the men's room. "Stay here. I'd like to talk to you."

"Bring some paper towels so I can mop up the floor!" She crouched down and gathered the mail she'd dropped, thankful the coffee hadn't soaked it. Then, it hit her.

Her boss had *kissed* her.

For a moment, she relived pressing herself up against that wall of solid muscle. And now he was stripping in the men's room.

Shit. He'd tell her it was a mistake and they couldn't be together unless she got another job. But she wasn't about to drop her job just because her boss kissed her silly.

"You know, if you wanted me to take my shirt off, all you have to do is ask."

Jade was grateful for the melanin that kept the heat in her face hidden. "Wh-what? Aiden, don't play switcheroo on me!"

"Aiden's not here." So it really was Andrew who was flirting with her while he strolled back into the office, closing the last of his buttons. He held paper towels, but instead of handing them to her, he kneeled and soaked up as much of the stain from the carpet as he could.

"You sure you're okay?" They asked each other at the same time, then laughed.

"I'm fine, Jade. How long had you had that cup of coffee? It was barely warm."

She shrugged. "Not sure. I stopped on the way here. It must have cooled off." This could have been the day from hell. "What did you want to talk about?"

"Did you mention anything to your friends about the attacker?"

That was not what she predicted. "No. You said you didn't want that to get out."

"I don't. But I thought one of them might offer to come pick you up after work."

Jade shook her head. "I can't ask that of them. It's too far out of the way."

He licked his lips. "I'll drive you home, then."

She blinked rapidly as her mouth went dry. "You don't need to."

"I want to. At least until they catch this asshole." He reached out and drew her hands into his as she got lost in his eyes. "Security shifts won't start until six, and you're done at five. Let me do this. It has the added bonus of getting me out of the office earlier. And maybe I could... take you to dinner?"

Was he for real? "Andrew... you're my *boss.*" Her heart beat faster inside her chest.

"My mother is planning to change your chain of command. By the end of today, you'll officially report directly to her, not me." When she opened her mouth to protest, he laid a finger over her lips. "Your job is secure, Jade. I promise."

If she'd had a decent night's sleep, she would throw off his hand. That was why she was weak in the knees. At least, that's what she told herself. "What are you saying?"

He let his touch drift down her arm. "You seemed interested in me the night we met. Is that still true?"

"I... er... how do you expect me to answer that?" Jade huffed out a laugh to hide her nerves.

One side of his lips lifted in amusement. "The truth, Jade. Always."

The truth? She'd lost several nights of sleep thinking about that Greek god body with the gentleman's manners, and she had spent most of the long weekend lamenting her decision not to text him the day after they met. But she couldn't tell him all of that. She was sure he'd bolt.

"I'm still interested." Her voice came out in a whisper.

"Are you free for dinner tonight?"

She nodded.

"Good." He leaned forward and whispered in her ear. "I desperately want to kiss you again, but I will get nothing done if I do."

Jade felt the butterflies take flight in her stomach once more. This time they were wearing tap shoes.

He pulled back then. "I'll be ready at five. Where do you like to eat?"

He expected her to think?

"My friends and I mostly go to Fabled." When he looked at her quizzically, she continued. "It's basically a sports bar, but for nerds."

He grinned. "Sounds fun, but loud."

She shrugged; he wasn't wrong.

"Anything you don't prefer?"

"Not especially."

"Do you eat seafood?"

Now she rolled her eyes. "Sugar, I'm from Louisiana. I *love* seafood."

Andrew visibly shuddered from head to toe. "Say that again."

"I love seafood?"

"No." He licked his lips. "What you called me."

"Sugar?"

Another shudder. "The way you say that is sexy as fuck."

Jade cocked an eyebrow. "I call everybody 'sugar.'"

He pulled her hands into his and squeezed them, heat dancing in his eyes. "You make it very difficult to control myself."

She stared at him, absorbing this enlightening information.

"We'll go to Fabled on a later date. I want this to be just for us."

Her heart hammered in her chest. That liquid steel gaze was doing funny things to her insides. "O—okay. I better get back to work, then." She backed away in a daze, then turned and walked towards his office door.

"I'll be here."

She pinched herself the minute she returned to her desk. *Not a dream.*

⸎

Andrew couldn't hold his grin when Jade's eyes widened as they drove up to the Orange Blossom's entrance. After helping her from the car, he passed the keys to the valet and took her hand.

"Matt said they've been booked up so quickly. How did you…"

"It helps to know the assistant manager," he replied with a wink.

Jade chuckled. "I walked into that one."

He pulled the industrial metal and glass door open and held it for her. Then they bypassed a large group of people waiting.

A short girl with a dark ponytail stood at the podium. "Good evening. Is it just the two of you?"

"Yes, I have a reservation; the name is Monroe."

The maitre'd lit up when she found them on the list. "Your table is ready. Follow me, please."

She led them to a booth in a side room where they could watch the marina from their perch by the window. Matt must have hand-picked this table himself, in the quietest, most intimate corner.

Jade sat in her chair and Andrew pushed it in.

"Is Matt working tonight?"

"He didn't mention it, so I'm not sure."

She shook her braids. "I am so going to hear about this in the group chat," she murmured as she studied the menu.

"Hmm?" He took a sip from the glass of water already on the table.

Jade chuckled. "We have a squad text thread. I think we've had it running since graduation. It was easier to communicate that way once we didn't live together anymore."

Andrew furrowed his brows in confusion. "What does that have to do with Matt?"

Jade snorted. "Matt has no secrets from Rosie, and Rosie will want to know what happened."

"Ahh." That made more sense. Then a thought occurred to him. "Isn't he younger than her?"

She shrugged. "Only by two years. Hardly a big deal in our twenties."

He was getting an idea of his date's age. Did Jade notice how old he was?

"What *would* be a significant age difference to you?"

"Well, if he was under eighteen, obviously."

"Of course. But I meant for you."

Jade's expression twisted in confusion. "What are you dancing around?"

He scrubbed a hand down his face. "Jade, I'm thirty-five. I just wanted to know if that was going to be an issue for you."

Her mouth dropped open, and she stared. Right then, their server arrived to take their order. After she'd ordered the blackened fish special, and he requested some delicious-sounding crab cakes, they resumed their discussion.

"You're kidding. I only pegged you for thirty, maybe."

He shrugged. "I get that sometimes."

She gazed out of the window at the boats bobbing in the bay. He hadn't meant to shock her, just try to figure out if this was going to be a problem.

While he waited for her to process, he sipped at his water. His mouth had gone dry. Was the difference that vast?

"I'm only twenty-five," she whispered.

Andrew's eyebrows disappeared into his hairline. "You carry yourself as if you were much older. Even older than your friends."

Jade shrugged. "I had to grow up fast, I guess."

When their salad course came, Andrew decided he should probably change the subject. "Where are you from in Louisiana?"

"I was born in Slidell, but I moved to New Orleans when I was sixteen." She didn't meet his eyes. A first date was not the time to unearth all her secrets, as much as he'd love to.

"When did you move to Baltimore?"

"I went to college here. I wasn't sure if I wanted to stay near my grandmother, but I got a scholarship for the University of Maryland. And it's good to leave the town that knew you before you changed your name."

He had heard from friends about how transitions often worked. Of course, Jade wouldn't stick around where she'd be recognized and deadnamed.

"Are you close to your grandma?"

Her smile lit up the room. "We are. She has always been my rock, my biggest supporter. I don't get to see her nearly enough, but we talk every week." A shadow crossed her face. "Well, almost every week. She hasn't picked up the last couple of times and I'm worried."

"Is she okay?"

"I'm not sure. She made a comment in passing about doctors but she said everything was fine and wouldn't tell me anything else."

He reached for her hand, needing to take that concerned expression from her face. "I'm certain she'll call you soon."

Jade gave him a sad smile that didn't reach her eyes. Her face said that she appreciated the attempt to cheer her up, but she doubted him. "What about you? Are you from here?"

"Nope. I grew up in Fairfax, Virginia, but my dad was transferred here when I was fifteen. We've lived here ever since."

Their entrees arrived and for a few minutes the only sounds they made were hums of appreciation for the food.

"You mentioned you used to read *X-Men*. Are you aware of the new series?"

"*Immortal X-Men*? I've heard about it but I haven't read anything. Is it good?"

Andrew launched into a spoiler-free speech about how ambitious the series was, how the politics had changed, and how the artwork had remained true to the original but updated for the modern era. "It's still *X-Men,* but clearly for an adult audience. It's absolutely amazing."

"Sure sounds that way." Her fork lay forgotten next to her half-eaten meal and her chin rested in her hand. "I'll have to get caught up."

"I have all of them if you want to read it."

"That's so sweet of you." Jade bit her lip and went back to her fish.

"It's completely selfish on my part. I'd love to discuss it with you." He grinned. Having all his attention on her was more intoxicating than any wine. "Who was your favorite character?"

Jade licked her lips. "I had two; Storm and Rogue."

"Really? I thought you'd say Gambit." Andrew made an attempt at a Cajun accent when he continued. "After all, he's de one from Louisiana."

She made a face of disgust. "Hell no, Gambit was an asshole. Not only was he a thief, he's the one that let the marauders into the Morlock tunnels and caused that huge mutant massacre in issue #350."

"Hey, he had no idea what Sinister had planned. And he tried to do better."

"I realize that, but I can't just claim him as a favorite. I prefer intelligent characters."

She certainly had him there; Gambit had been kind of dumb in the beginning.

Jade glanced at him from beneath her lashes. "That extends to real life as well."

Holy shit, she was flirting with him! His chest warmed at the compliment.

"Same goes for me." Her eyelashes fluttered as she stared down at her food.

They lingered over dessert until the stars started coming out, but dinner was over far too quickly for him. Andrew wanted to draw the evening out and keep talking to her.

"Why don't we take a walk along the water?"

But Jade shook her head, the corners of her mouth turned down. "I'd love to, but I have to get up stupid early in the morning to make my bus, and my feet still aren't used to dress shoes."

Andrew's brows furrowed. "How long does it take you to get to work?"

Jade shrugged as they made their way over to his car. "About an hour, depending on whether the bus is on time."

That sounded terrible. The drive was only thirty minutes with traffic. He sped ahead to get to her door before her, since she apparently intended to open it herself.

Andrew cleared his throat as he grabbed the handle right before she did. "I could drive you."

She shook her head. "No, thanks. I like taking the bus."

Andrew shrugged and closed her door after he was sure she was tucked safely inside. Then he rounded the Explorer and slid into his seat. "Is it a saving-the-environment thing?"

"Well, I won't deny that's nice, too." She turned in her seat, pointing her knees at him in that dark gray skirt. "But no. It's more of a seeing-the-city thing." Long, dark fingers encircled his. "Are you okay?"

He smiled and turned his hand over, lacing their fingers together, and looked into her dark eyes. "I don't want tonight to be over."

"Me neither." She stared at where their hands were linked.

Andrew released her, teasing over her fingers as he reluctantly withdrew. This close, he watched her shiver as goosebumps popped up on her arms. As soon as they were out of the parking lot, Andrew dropped his hand to hers once more, tracing gentle circles over her wrist. They sat in contented silence all the way to her apartment building.

Sighing, Andrew put the SUV in park and leaned back in his seat, turning to face Jade. She smiled and played her fingers across his again. "Walk me up?"

He grinned and brought her hand to his lips. "Absolutely."

This time, she waited for him to open her door. They walked arm-in-arm to the black metal and glass door, then held hands as they walked up the steps to her second-floor apartment. Yet again, they arrived at their destination all too soon. Jade unlocked her door and turned to face him.

"Thanks for dinner," she murmured. "I had a great time."

"Me too. Can I see you again?"

His question was met with a flirty smile. "You'll see me at work tomorrow."

"I meant outside of the office."

"You mean another date?"

"Is that so shocking? I like you, Jade."

Her brow furrowed. "For starters, you've been giving me mixed signals since I started at the Unicorn."

He grimaced. "I'm sorry. I tried to stay away because I didn't want to make you uncomfortable." Andrew chuckled. "I really thought I could fight this attraction."

She smiled sadly at him. "It's not just that."

"Hmm?" He waited for her to continue. Her tongue darted out to moisten her lips.

And now he wanted to lean in and kiss her, but he needed to hear what she had to say more.

"Most men find me intimidating, you know." Her brown eyes gazed at him from under her thick lashes. She was slouching, just a bit, and he hated that she felt the need to make herself smaller.

"Because of your height? Or because they don't know what to do with you in bed?"

"The second one, for sure. Most of the guys in college were straight with no wiggle room, and telling them about myself didn't always end well. But even when they were in the dark about it, they seemed... off."

"Ah. Because you're intelligent, tall, and beautiful." Her eyelashes kissed her cheekbones as she looked away. "I think you'll find I'm not most men, Jade."

She nodded, and visibly straightened her back, lifting her head at the same time so they were eye-to-eye. "I'm learning that."

His hand rose of its own accord to cup her jaw. "May I kiss you again?"

Her response was a breathy whisper. "Please."

Gently, oh so tenderly, he pressed his lips to hers. Her arms encircled his neck as she sighed, and he slipped his tongue inside to taste her mouth. He wrapped her in a tight embrace as they lost themselves in each other. Their tongues teased each other in a slow, seductive dance. Time was meaningless; there was only Jade and this kiss.

A whistle from down the hall broke the spell, followed by a door closing. Jade pulled away, and Andrew chased her mouth with his until she pressed against his chest. "I should have mentioned Nadia lives on the same floor as me." She winced. "My phone is about to blow up."

He grinned. "Tell the squad I said hi, and I'll see you tomorrow." As much as he wanted to, if he kissed her again, he'd have to drive with an erection, and that did not sound like fun.

"Text me when you get home?"

"Sure." He walked backwards towards the stairs until she opened her door and slipped inside to watch him.

"Good night," she called quietly.

"Sweet dreams." Then he turned and jogged down the staircase, so he didn't turn around and go back to her.

Chapter 9

Jade: I have a problem.

Olivia: What's up?

Nadia: Do I need to hurt someone?
Or call my brothers?

Jade: No, no, nothing like that. I'm not even sure how much of an issue this should be.

Rosie: Is something wrong?

Jade: Andrew told me how old he is.

Mia: Okay…

Jade: He's ten years older than me.

Olivia: Seriously?

Nadia: I never would have guessed that.

Jade: Me neither!

Rosie: Does it bother you?

Jade: I can't decide. Should it? Won't his family think I'm too young for him?

Mia: Well, it's not up to us to judge. And it's not up to them, either. Mom dated guys older AND younger than her, and she always told me age had nothing to do with compatibility. All that matters is that you two are happy and take care of each other.

Jade: He seems to have a different idea of what that looks like. But I'm not sure if that's his age or something else.

Rain splattered the concrete beneath her flats as Jade hurried to the bus stop. The 5:10 always arrived on time and had the shortest route to the transfer point. She would take a second bus from there to her own neighborhood. Sliding under the glass roof of MTA's bus shelter, she brushed water from her green satin blouse. At least she hadn't worn white today. She made a mental note to keep an umbrella at her desk.

She didn't hear Andrew's footsteps over the noise of the traffic on the street, so when he tapped her on her shoulder, she almost jumped out of her skin. "Andrew! Did I forget something?"

"What are you doing?" He scowled at her.

"Waiting for the bus, of course." What did it look like she was doing?

"Baby, I can drive you home."

"But... I just saw you yesterday. We didn't make any plans."

"It's not safe. They still haven't caught Ember's attacker." He drew close until his black umbrella covered both their heads. He was too young to look so grumpy. Without thinking, she reached out and smoothed the wrinkle between his brows with her thumb.

"I'll be fine." She looked to her left. Even now, she could see her bus creeping its way along the busy street. "My bus is right there."

"You take it straight home?"

"Well, no. I have to transfer."

That wrinkle was back, and he had a frown to go along with it. "You don't have an umbrella."

"I know, I forgot it. But I won't melt."

"Just let me drive you, Jade. Please?"

Memories of his goodnight kiss last night made her heartbeat race. Jade bit her lip, eyeing the bus that was a block closer now, and the rain coming down harder.

"I'll worry the whole time." His scowl had disappeared and in its place were puppy eyes of molten steel that Jade found she couldn't refuse. "My Explorer is right back there."

It was now or never. She grasped onto his outstretched hand. "Alright, sugar." Those glorious dimples came out from behind the clouds when he smiled at her. He led her out from under the MTA shelter and towards the fenced in parking lot outside the club.

Andrew opened the passenger door to his black SUV, and she slid inside. He dumped the umbrella into the back before getting into the driver's seat.

Jade had to admit that his vehicle was far more comfortable than the bus, and the company was better, too. Stopping in traffic was a lot more fun when he reached over to hold her hand.

They talked about everything: Aidan's antics at Sunday dinner when their mom had finally pulled out the baby books, funny stories from college, and their favorite places in Baltimore. All too soon, Andrew parked outside the Mason Hollow Apartments.

"You don't have to walk me up again."

"But I want to." He leaned over, his voice low and seductive. "And it's easier to kiss you goodnight in the hall."

Jade felt her pulse flutter in her throat. "Okay then." Who was she to complain that this hunk wanted to kiss her again?

Andrew turned off the car. "Wait here." He pulled the umbrella out from the backseat and walked around to her car door, then opened it with the umbrella over their heads so that she wouldn't get wet. Sliding out of the Explorer and pushing her purse up her shoulder, Jade took his arm, and they walked across the lot. She unlocked the outside door, and he followed her up the stairs to her apartment, which didn't surprise her.

After opening her door and turning around, she expected him to kiss her and go home. Instead, he took her chin between his fingers so he could look into her eyes. "I'm bringing you home every night, Jade."

"Andrew, that's really not—"

"I need this. Please, Jade."

He had a seriousness in his face she couldn't ignore. And behind that was... fear. Jade sighed. Would it really hurt anything?

"Alright—" She barely got the word out before he took her mouth in a fierce kiss. One arm banded around her back and the other held her head as his tongue explored every crevice of her mouth. Jade clutched his shirt from behind and was swept away by the tide.

Footsteps on the stairs snapped her out of her daze, and she hesitantly broke away from him. "Maybe you should come inside."

Andrew shook his head. "Didn't you say you were calling Memaw tonight?"

Shit, he was right. She had been anxious about Memaw for a while. Her grandmother had been missing more phone calls than she answered. Something was wrong. Jade could feel it in her gut.

Andrew laid a sweet kiss on her cheek. "If I come in now, we won't stop. Want to go out again on Friday?"

"Let me check with the girls." Fridays were usually girls' nights, but with her squad pairing off, they'd been less frequent. But Andrew seemed adamant about spending her free time with her.

It filled her with flattery.

He nodded. "Let me know, okay?" Then, as if he couldn't help himself, he laid one more kiss on her lips, soft and lingering. "I'll text you when I get home."

"Okay." She leaned into the doorjamb as he walked away, and didn't shut herself inside until he'd disappeared down the stairs.

Leaning back against the door, Jade fanned herself with her hand. God*damn*, she was a lucky woman.

But first, Memaw.

Jade lifted the cell phone to her ear and waited for her grandmother to pick up. Unfortunately, she got the answering machine.

"Hi, you've reached Lou Ellen. Please leave your name and number and I will return your call as soon as possible. Au re'oir!"

Sighing as the machine beeped, Jade left another message.

"Memaw, it's me, Jade. I miss you. Call me back as soon as you can. Love you more."

Jade clicked to hang up and then slumped onto her couch. Her heart ached to tell Memaw about Andrew. Maybe she'd have some advice for her regarding this baffling man.

Chapter 10

It had taken a lot of convincing, or as Jade referred to it, nagging, but Andrew had finally persuaded Jade to let him drive her to work this morning. Apparently, a white lie about a traffic detour taking him by her apartment was enough. He parked behind The Neon Unicorn and ran around to open Jade's door for her. She had a habit of not waiting for him, just to mess with his head. They'd turned it into a race.

"Fine, you beat me." Jade took his hand and gave him a small smile, which he returned tenfold. She let him win, but he was smart enough not to point that out.

They dodged the usual sidewalk traffic together and slipped into the club, parting ways with a kiss when she reached her desk.

Andrew unloaded his laptop bag and stopped in the break room for coffee before heading into his twin's office. "Morning."

"Hello," Aiden grunted.

"Long shift?"

"You know it." His twin took a sip of his own brew and pulled a chair up to his desk. "Our security team saw someone hanging around the bus stop late last night. I have the camera footage ready to roll; you want to watch it?"

"Hell yeah. Let me go down and see if Ember's available to ID this guy." At Aiden's nod, he jogged downstairs and shortly returned with Ember.

He gestured for Ember to take the chair next to Aiden, and Andrew stood behind them.

"You okay?" Aiden asked their friend.

She nodded, her fists clenched on her thighs. "Let's find out if this is our man."

Aiden pressed play on the computer screen, and the grainy nighttime footage began.

A nondescript white male in a hoodie came up to the bus stop with his hands in his pockets, nervously looking around.

"It's kinda hard to tell if that's him." Ember breathed a sigh of relief. Her bruises may have healed, but Andrew knew her shoulder still bothered her. He hated asking her to look at the footage, but they couldn't just send a video of a public bus shelter to the police without reason.

Right then on the screen, one of the security guards at The Neon Unicorn walked by under the camera, and the man in the hooded sweatshirt scurried away.

"That looks suspicious." Aiden stopped the playback.

"It does. But I'd need a closer look to be sure." Ember chewed on her thumbnail.

They were out of options. "At least we've got our guys as a deterrent. Without a positive identification, there's nothing the police will do."

"That's not good enough." Jade strolled into the room, snagging Andrew's attention away from the monitor. "He hurt one of our own and we need to put him behind bars."

"We can't install a camera in a public bus shelter. That's the only way it could get close enough."

"What if we moved it down, instead of leaving it on the roofline?"

Aiden pursed his lips. "Now you're talking. Let me call my guy and ask him to come out here. If we do this quickly, we might catch this asshole before he strikes again." Aiden pulled out his cell and dialed someone as the rest of them left the room.

"I'm sorry, Andrew. I wish I could tell if it was him."

"Don't worry about it. We'll keep trying."

"You okay to work tonight, sugar?" Jade asked. She'd taken Ember on as another friend and Andrew's heart melted. She had been so understanding of Ember's situation, checking up on her and eating lunch with her. And the fierce manner in which she demanded justice for his buddy made his cock hard.

She might call everyone "sugar". But it sounded different when she said it to him and he loved it.

Jade had a way of putting people at ease, but she didn't seem to recognize it in herself. Soon Ember returned downstairs to help Colin stock the bar, and Aiden emerged from his office.

"Scott's going to come back and move the camera today before we open. With any luck, we'll catch this guy tonight."

Andrew nodded. "Thanks for the idea, Jade."

Her eyelashes fluttered as she looked away. "I like Ember. And this asshole needs to go to jail."

His lungs expanded with pride, along with his smile. "I'm glad. And I never would have thought about something as simple as moving the camera."

She shrugged.

"Don't do that." He lifted her chin. "Do not minimize your contribution. We're a team. The Neon Unicorn is a family and we look out for each other. And you're part of it."

Her eyes shone at him with an emotion he couldn't name. But he didn't need to. He laid a soft, chaste kiss on her lips and backed away. "See you at lunch, baby."

Nadia: How often is that man going to bring you home after work?

Jade: Are you keeping tabs on me?

Rosie: It's so sweet. He's done it every day for weeks now. Why would he stop?

Nadia: So, this is a permanent thing?

Jade: Not exactly.

Olivia: What do you mean?

Jade: There was an… incident at the club. And he's concerned about me taking the bus. So until they arrest the perpetrator, he wants to drive me home.

Mia: That doesn't sound good.

Jade: It's not, but we don't want anything to get out. Aiden beefed up security and they're hoping to catch him soon.

Rosie: Your boyfriend is super thoughtful.

Jade: He's my boss.

Mia: Why can't he be both?

Jade squirmed in Andrew's front seat, the text conversation with her squad making her wonder that herself. Every night since their first date, he'd driven her home and laid an electrifying kiss on her at her door.

She was grateful that Ember was back at work. Her injuries had mostly healed, although she couldn't lift cases like she used to. Her attacker remained at large, so Andrew still acted super protective. Jade thought it would have faded by now with no move from the assailant. At some point, he needed to let her live her life.

"Everything okay?" Andrew asked from the driver's seat.

"I'm afraid you're spoiling me." She tried to joke.

He looked over at her and winked one gray eye. "Maybe that's the idea."

She stayed silent. Jade didn't lean on anyone, not even her friends, for much. She'd learned early on that the only person she could count on was herself. The only people who hadn't walked away from her completely were Memaw and her squad.

And with the squad, it was only a matter of time.

"You never answered me about our next date. What do you want to do?"

She had no plans for the night. Everyone else was either working or spending the evening with their significant others. Girls' night was all but forgotten. So why shouldn't she have a date with her hot boss? Or whatever he was at this point. Even if he was driving her a little nuts.

"I'm not busy tonight. But I don't want to go anywhere; I'm too tired."

"How about takeout? Chinese?"

Her stomach growled loud enough to be heard over the traffic. "Kung Pao shrimp sounds amazing right now. Do you want to eat at my place?"

"Sounds good to me. Where should we order from?"

"Golden Crane is on the way."

"Are they on GrubHub?"

"I think so."

Andrew handed her his phone from the cupholder. "Here, order whatever you want for pick up. My card's saved in the app."

Wow. Jade was humbled by his trust in her. His phone opened the minute her thumb swiped across the screen. "No password?" He had to be smarter than that.

Andrew just laughed. "When it's hooked up to my car's Bluetooth, it doesn't ask for one. It makes things easier when I need to check the GPS app."

"Ooh, fancy." Scrolling to the app, she pulled up the restaurant and started her order. Kung Pao shrimp, some egg rolls, fried rice... "What do you want?"

His deep chuckle flooded her with warmth. "That's a loaded question."

Resisting the urge to fan herself, Jade pointed at the screen. "I meant to eat."

"Still a loaded question."

God damn. Jade pretended to be annoyed. "What do you want me to order for you from the restaurant?"

Andrew's dimples popped with his grin. "Do they have hot fish?"

She scrolled down and found the dish he asked for. "Yep. What kind of rice?"

"White rice, please."

"I was going to order egg rolls. That work for you?"

He lifted her free hand to his mouth and pressed a quick kiss to her knuckles. "Perfect."

They swung by the Golden Crane and picked up their order on the way back to Mason Hollow Apartments. The car filled with the delicious scent of fried food, and Jade's mouth watered. Her stomach growled. Taking the stairs at breakneck speed, they finally arrived at her door.

As soon as she got the door open and went inside, Jade slid out of her shoes with a sigh. Then she pulled out silverware from her tiny galley kitchen while Andrew lifted containers of food and set them on her second-hand coffee table.

She slipped onto the couch next to him, ready to eat, but her cell rang. It was Memaw!

"I have to take this, sorry." Andrew cocked his head to one side and furrowed his brows.

"Memaw! It's been ages. Where've you been?"

A cough greeted her over the phone before her grandmother spoke. "I've been busy, child. I hated missing our weekly calls."

"Did you get my message about the new job?"

"Yes!" Her voice was thin and reedy, and she didn't sound like herself. "I'm so proud of you, Jade. How is it?"

"It's great. Everyone is really nice, and I don't have to be on my feet making drinks anymore." Jade looked over her shoulder at Andrew apologetically. She hated to do this when she was supposed to be spending time with him. "Are you feeling okay?"

"I feel fine." Memaw coughed again.

"You don't sound very good."

"The fall allergies hit me hard. That's all this is."

Memaw had never lied to Jade before in her whole life. Something was wrong. But she couldn't keep talking to Memaw like this, with Andrew sitting next to her, waiting to eat his meal.

"Can I call you later, Memaw? I have someone over for dinner."

Lou Ellen's voice brightened. "You have a date?"

"I, uh..." She glanced at Andrew from the corner of her eye. "Yes. I met somebody. At work."

She practically squealed. "I can't wait to hear about him, child! I'll be right here. You have a good time. Love you!"

"Love you more, Memaw. Bye now." Jade hung up, that sinking feeling in her gut returning. Or maybe that was just her hunger.

"How's Memaw?" Andrew asked, passing her the shrimp she'd ordered.

"She claims she's fine. But she's not telling me something, and that's been driving me nuts."

Andrew threw an arm around her shoulders. The weight of it settled her stomach and helped her relax. "If something's wrong, she'll tell you when she's ready. Until then, you can really only accept what she says at face value."

"I know. But it's bothering me." She popped a shrimp into her mouth, and they ate in silence until Andrew set his containers down and leaned over.

His lips nibbled at her ear as she finished her dinner. "Let me take your mind off it?"

She sank willingly into his husky voice and muscular arms. Those kisses he'd given her daily for the last two weeks had only whetted her appetite, and inspired some steamy fantasies. Nothing else mattered when his mouth met hers and their tongues danced together. And here on her couch, they weren't limited to just one.

Andrew's kisses were addicting; she couldn't stop.

A groan slipped from her throat as Andrew's tongue painted down one side of her neck, then up the other side.

"Jade," he murmured in that voice that gave her goosebumps. "Tell me to stop."

"Don't stop." He felt good, too good, taking her out of her head and turning her into a pile of mush. She chased his mouth with hers and latched on with her whole body, straddling him on her couch. He'd teased her enough. Her braids formed a curtain around them, shutting out the world.

When she came up for air, Andrew's hands slid up her back under her top.

"Is this okay?"

A sly grin split her swollen lips. "Can I take yours off too?"

He groaned in answer, and in seconds her palms were roaming his muscular pecs and an eight-pack of abs. "You were holding out on me, sugar. Hiding those muscles under that wardrobe."

Andrew smirked as he cupped her breasts in his big hands. "You don't like surprises?"

"Mmm, in this case, I love them." Jade leaned forward and pressed their chests together as she gave his neck the same treatment he'd given hers. Soon she was grinding down on the pipe in his pants and listening to his gasps.

One warm hand slid down the back of her jeans, and the other hovered around her bra clasp. "Jade..."

"Andrew," she purred, nipping his earlobe and delighting in his shudder. "If the answer is no, I will stop you." She licked the spot she'd taken between her teeth to soothe it. "I'm ready for you."

That must have been what he was waiting to hear. Her undergarment went flying across the room and Jade cried out in shock when he sucked her whole damn boob into his mouth. Her nails dug into his shoulders as he made love to the sensitive flesh. She thought she'd come from that alone when he switched sides, but he flipped her on her back on the couch too fast. Then his warm tongue was traveling down, down, down, to where her jeans fastened. Looking up at her, Andrew maintained eye contact while he unbuttoned and unzipped her pants with his teeth. As he pulled them open, she froze in sudden fear.

She'd never told him what to expect down there.

Something in her expression gave her away, because Andrew shed his inner animal instantly. He rose on his knees and leaned over her, cradling her face in his hands. "Doesn't matter what I find, baby, I still want you. That will not change."

Her breathing slowed as his words relaxed her. "Did you know that the head of the penis and the clitoris start as the same cells in the womb?" Immediately, she cringed at her own word vomit. Her nerves had gotten the best of her.

"Is that what you call it?" He cocked his head to one side, his gaze never leaving hers.

"Sometimes."

Andrew nodded. "If you want to end it here, that's fine. I'll never push you."

Jade took a deep breath, shook her head, then picked his hands off her cheeks and placed them back on her hips. "Don't stop."

She'd been so... inspired... these last couple of weeks that she had started using her vibrator nightly, stretching herself so she could take him up her anus. The one she owned could hit her prostate most of the time, but a live human would be so much better than silicone.

With reverence, Andrew pulled her pants and panties down her legs slowly, appreciating the gift she offered him. Her heart pounded in her chest. Goosebumps erupted over her skin as he slid his hands up her naked thighs.

He stood up and shucked the rest of his clothes, revealing an enormous cock that made her vibrator look tiny in comparison. Then he laid down over her on the couch, his legs hanging over the arm because of his height. Jade swallowed a laugh.

"Should we move to my bedroom?"

Andrew looked like he was thinking about it, then stood once more. "That would probably be a smart idea. What I want to do requires a bit more room."

"Good thing I have a queen bed," she quipped back as she rose.

"Should be goddess-size."

Jade laughed. "I don't think one of those would fit in here. So I'll make do."

Her mattress took up most of the space in her bedroom, but at least the closet was large. Andrew followed her down and kissed her again. They laid like that, skin to skin, mouths in a mating dance, until Jade was breathless.

When he started licking another line down her neck and then continued down between her breasts, he had a request. "Show me how you touch yourself."

Jade's hands flew to the secret channels on either side of her sex and rubbed. Andrew hovered over her for a few minutes, just watching, his hot breath tickling her clit. Then he lowered his mouth over it while she was still going, his tongue dancing over her girl-dick. Lightning jolted through her veins, and soon every muscle in her body tensed as the best orgasm of her life washed over her.

She pushed his face from her crotch once she'd come down from her high, gasping. "Damn, sugar." He shot a well-deserved grin full of pride at her. "Your turn now."

Andrew shook his dreadlocks as he stretched out beside her. "I don't need anything."

She reached down, grabbed his dick, and began to slide her hand up and down. He threw his head back with a groan. "This club between your legs seems to disagree."

"I... I.... oh God, that feels so good."

He was so long, Jade knew he was going to hit her P-spot perfectly. "I want you in my ass."

Andrew's eyes opened in a snap. "Really?"

She nodded and slid her tongue into his mouth in a sensual kiss as she continued to stroke him slowly. "You're bigger than my vibrator, but I'd like to try."

"I'll go slow." He slipped from her grasp and tumbled off the bed. "I have a condom in my wallet. Let me grab it." She would have protested, but watching that beautiful ass run out of her bedroom made the wait worth it.

While he got the condom, Jade reached into her bedside table and pulled out her lube. He walked back in as he was stretching the latex barrier over his thick cock. She handed him the bottle, and he slicked up his dick. Then he used his lube-soaked fingers to gently circle her rim.

Jade whimpered at his teasing touch, which turned to a whine as he slipped first one, then two digits inside.

"Gotta stretch you, baby. Don't want to hurt you."

"So good." She arched on the bed as he scissored his fingers inside her ass, then added a third. "Please."

"As my Goddess commands." He held her ass open as the thick head of his cock pressed against her rosebud. She pushed down until it popped past the ring of muscle, and then he slid inch by inch into her channel.

Dear God. She'd never felt so full. Andrew was going to ruin her vibrator for her. Sweat dripped down his face as he inched inside her. When he finally sank all the way in, his tip nudged her P-spot and she knew she was in for the best sex of her life.

Chapter 11

ANDREW FINALLY BOTTOMED OUT in Jade's tight ass, his blood pounding in his ears. He didn't want to hurt her, but he knew from previous lovers that taking him in the butt was no small feat. Most partners that were into anal needed to work up to it. But from what she said on the couch, she must have been preparing herself for this. Knowing how much she wanted him turned him on like nothing else.

It had been ages since Andrew last took a partner to bed, not that he could think of anyone specific right now. Jade had made him forget all his other lovers. He gripped her hips, dragged himself back, then thrust inside once more.

He started out slow, but when she cried out, "That's the spot! Harder!" it was difficult not to speed up. The slap of skin on skin and their gasping breaths filled the night air.

He wanted to bottle this moment so it would last forever. Then fireworks danced behind his eyes as he exploded into the condom, and Jade screamed out her own climax.

Andrew hovered over her, his softening dick still in her ass. She glowed beneath him. "You're so beautiful." He drank in her smile, sipping from her lips as he slipped from her. "I'll be right back."

The bathroom was easy to find, and once he cleaned himself up and got rid of the condom, he gently wiped Jade with a damp washcloth, then threw it in her hamper. He crawled back into bed and pulled her into his arms.

"Shower?" she croaked.

He could barely move. "How about in the morning?"

"Sounds good." Her head laid over his chest, and Andrew wondered what the hell he had done in his life to deserve her.

"Why am I looking at houses with you instead of your girlfriend?" Jade asked Mia as they piled into her hot pink Mini Cooper after her day at the Neon Unicorn was over.

"Because Marcia has a team-building thing with the Casa crew." Mia turned the ignition over. "Which translates to getting food and talking shop. But Eddie insisted she go to this one."

"So why not schedule this for another time?"

"Because she's kind of sick of looking at houses with me." A blush rose to Mia's fair cheeks. "I don't think she understands how loaded my grandparents were, and she doesn't realize we can afford a place like the one I want to get."

Jade massaged her temples as a headache tried to grab hold. "Just promise me you won't try to surprise her with a house. Look at this one and then take her there as well?"

"That's exactly what I'm doing." Mia turned the wheel. "You have an expert eye and know me like a sister. I'll snap photos and when I show her how little it's going to cost us month to month, then she'll go see it with me."

"She's getting sticker shock?"

"Every time." She shook her blonde head. "We've talked and talked about our house wish list. And we need the space for when her siblings come to visit. Not to mention we want kids of our own."

Jade smiled softly. Mia had effectively been an only child growing up, so it made sense for her to plan for a big family.

"So why this place?"

"It's not too far from Eddie's shop, there's four bed-rooms, walk-in closets, and the primary has an en suite."

"When was it built?"

"About ten years ago."

Jade hemmed and hawed. "I can't see Marcia being happy with a McMansion."

"But it's so nice! And the backyard is perfect for parties. We can put up a swing set and everything."

It was a good thing Mia had brought her. She came from a background similar to Marcia's — she might not have shared a bedroom in an apartment with her sister, but her family also hadn't had money for expensive things.

They arrived at a home in a gated neighborhood. Three stories of light gray siding greeted them with a perfect, manicured landscape.

"How on earth will you be able to tell your house apart? They all look the same."

Mia waved her off. "We can put a sign out front."

And what would their neighbors think about a queer couple moving into the area? Jade worried their future children wouldn't feel welcome. Plus, Casa crew parties were loud, and she could already hear the cops at the door.

But she walked through the building with Mia, anyway.

Her realtor gushed at every turn, pointing out the large walk-in pantry and dual ovens. All stuff that Mia could put into another house if she wanted. Same with the double vanity in the primary bath.

"The yard doesn't have a fence." Jade pointed out. "You wouldn't be able to let the kids out without supervision."

"I could always put one up."

While she took the tour with her friend, Jade downloaded a house hunter's app to her phone. She had a better idea of what Marcia would be comfortable with, and Mia still had months to go on her lease. They might as well make use of the time.

Mia told the realtor she'd be in touch and got back into the car with Jade. "So, what did you think?"

"The ceilings are high, which sounds great unless it's winter, or until you have a loud party and the echoes get to you. The finishes are nice, but the yard isn't private at *all*, and you'd be a queer multicultural couple moving into a suburban white bread neighborhood. Mia, I love you like a sister, but are you *nuts*?"

Mia's face fell. "I hadn't considered that."

Jade gentled her tone. "I can't imagine Marcia in that house at all. And most of the things you liked about it can be put into an older home and done to your exact tastes. Instead of the boring box that place was." Mia had way too much personality to squeeze into a home like that.

"What are you saying?"

"You guys need a house with character. Somewhere you can do your own thing. Where Eddie can paint a mural in the kids' playroom and not have it feel out of place." Just then, Jade found what she was looking for in the app. *And* it had an open house today. She passed her phone over to Mia. "Look at this one. It's got plenty of space, it just needs sprucing up, and maybe some repair work. You could knock out this wall here and make a big kitchen and pantry if you want. Plus, the basement's a blank slate. You can turn it into a playroom, guest suite, or whatever you feel like."

"There are no close neighbors."

"There's also no homeowners' association that's going to come down on you for loud parties. And it has plenty of space for a football game before the woods begin."

"Alright, I'm in. Let's check out the open house and if I like it, then I'll text my realtor."

It was further away, but a separate three-car garage sat at the end of a long gravel driveway. A sprawling old Colonial style home greeted them in yellow brick and white columns. It reminded her a little of Memaw's home. Except for the people crawling all over the property.

"There's plenty of room for vehicles."

"Clearly. Lots of parking for parties." She grinned. They found a space next to a minivan and disembarked. Jade grabbed a flier by the front door while Mia ogled the grand foyer.

"Apparently, it used to be a funeral home." Jade read from the information packet.

"Wouldn't that put people off?"

"In this market? Probably not."

Formal parlors abounded, and there was a ton of carpet. The kitchenette was tiny, but they could convert the offices upstairs into bedrooms.

"This is a lot of work."

"You have most of the year left on your lease. You have time."

"I like the fireplaces."

"Yeah, they'll be fun to decorate at Christmas."

The basement had been the embalming lab, but the sellers had cleaned it out completely. It was a clean slate.

"At least they installed washer and dryer hookups." Jade noted the capped-off pipes with the tags stating they'd been inspected.

Mia stood in the center of the room and turned in a slow circle. "We could have a lot of fun designing this place."

Now she was getting the idea! "Put that budget towards the renovations. And you know the squad and crew would help with labor."

"Painting party?"

"Hell yeah, sugar."

Mia took tons of photos and sent the listing information to her realtor. Then they inspected the garage.

"Look at this space up here!"

Stairs at the back of the third bay led to a second level. "Oh good, you can store all the Christmas decorations you're going to buy for this place."

"Or..." Mia fidgeted.

"Or what?"

"Turn it into guest housing? Or an apartment! In case someone missed us."

Jade's brows furrowed. "What are you saying?"

"You could move with us!"

"Mia, I can't... I wouldn't do that to you. You will need your own space. I'm good with the apartments. Plus, the bus doesn't come all the way out here."

"Oh." Her friend scuffed the toe of her sneaker against the dusty subfloor.

"Why would you want me to live with you? You two are in love and you'll be in a new home. The last thing you need is a roommate."

"We're all moving out of the building and I just didn't want you to think I was abandoning you."

Jade reached out and hugged her friend. "We'll always be squad sisters. That's never going to change. But everyone needs to live their own lives, too. And it's not like you're leaving the city."

"At least you're making better money with the new job, right?"

"Yep. I'm doing fine." Warmth spread through her chest, knowing her friend would think to ask her to come along. It was gratifying to have someone at her back.

Mia's phone alerted her to a text. "Marcia likes it and wants to see it! She thinks it's funny that it used to be a funeral parlor."

"I thought it might speak to the morbid in her."

Laughing, Mia showed Jade her phone. "She's talking about covering a fireplace in skulls."

"I think they make gas inserts shaped like skulls instead of fake logs."

"Oh, my God! That would be perfect. We're going to need a *Dungeons and Dragons* room, anyway."

Now that was an idea. "You should decorate it like the tavern!"

"Nad will flip." Mia led her down the stairs.

"How will this work with your Barbie aesthetic?"

She shrugged. "I can use that in my office. Also, black goes with pink."

"True."

Her phone dinged again. "Eddie and the crew offered to help paint. And he says check under the carpet for hardwoods." Mia busied herself typing back.

"I told her she gets to design the dungeon for gaming if we keep the rest of the house in other colors."

"What did she say?"

They waited for another text. "Deal."

Now the wheels in her friend's head were turning. "We could put in a pool at some point when the kids were older."

"Epic!"

Mia spouted off ideas for the entire ride home, like consulting an engineer before they made an offer, so they knew ahead of time whether they could knock walls out. Jade smiled as Mia rambled. Maybe someday that would be her and Andrew.

Just then, her own phone sounded.

Andrew: Are you done yet?

Jade: We're on the way home now.

Andrew: Good. I can't wait to see you again.

Jade: I'm going to make Mia feed me first.

Andrew: But I can do that!

Jade: Yeah, but I think it's only fair for her to do it, given the situation.

Andrew: Tell her I want to meet you guys for dinner. Then I won't have to wait.

> Jade: Bossy.

Andrew: Yes, and?

> Jade: Fine, I'll ask her.

"Hey," Jade said, to get Mia's attention. "I'm starving. How do you feel about meeting Andrew for dinner? We have... plans tonight."

"Sure! Tell him to meet us at Fabled." Mia smirked and elbowed her in the ribs. "What *kind* of plans?"

"None of your business." Jade's face flushed.

"I'll warn Nadia. She might need earplugs."

"Brat," Jade said with a grin.

Mia turned to her as they sat at a red light. "Text him. I'm starved, too."

> Jade: Meet us at Fabled? Mia's hungry, too.

Andrew: See you soon, baby.

Jade smiled at her phone. "He'll meet us there."

"Fantastic. Think he'll cry at the dragon burger like Caleb did?"

"Hell no, sugar. My man can handle spice. He's dating *me*." Jade indicated herself with her hands as they both laughed.

Chapter 12

NUMBERS DANCED MERRILY INTO their places on the spreadsheet in front of him. The Neon Unicorn could be in the red, but it wouldn't faze Andrew right now. Nothing could ruin his perfect mood.

He'd slept over at Jade's place the last two nights. And she was sleeping over at his apartment tomorrow.

That first morning, he'd let her take the bus as usual, since he had to run home and change. But while he was there, he packed a bag. They'd made dinner together and cozied up in front of the television after work. Not that they'd paid a bit of attention to whatever had been on the screen.

She had a girls' night with her friends tonight, or he'd be looking for a third night in a row.

A light tapping on the door's frame brought Andrew's gaze up from his screen. When he saw Jade standing there, he grinned.

"Come in and shut the door behind you, baby." He rose from his desk and met her halfway across the room. She chucked the mail on the wooden surface and went willingly into his arms.

Andrew worshiped her mouth until she pulled away. "Geez, it's not like you just had me this morning or any-thing," she teased.

"But I have to go a whole night without you."

Jade rolled her dark brown eyes. "Aw, you'll survive."

"Don't forget your assigned reading, now."

She squealed in excitement. "I can't wait! I'm tempted to ditch the squad altogether and read all night."

Chuckling, he laid one more quick kiss on her lips. She'd about died when he unpacked his entire collection of *The Immortal X-Men* for her to borrow last night. "As eager as I am to hear what you think about it, I don't want you to cancel on your girls."

"Nah, I wouldn't actually do that." She kissed him again and grabbed a handful of his ass, making him groan as his cock came to attention.

"What you do to me, woman!" Sweat dripped into the collar of his Oxford shirt as his skin heated. Her lips trailed down his neck, evoking a shiver.

"Do you have any meetings?" Jade asked with that sultry rasp that turned him on so much. His only answer was to shake his head.

"Can you sit down? I wanna do something." Her long nails grazed over the front of his trousers, and the chubby he had been fighting became a full-blown erection. He'd do anything she wanted right now.

She guided him back into his desk chair, then she kneeled on the floor in her pencil skirt and slipped underneath. "Wha—what are you doing?" he stammered as she pulled him into place.

Scheming eyes glanced up at him from the shadows as her deft fingers opened his belt and slid his zipper down. "I read about this once and I've always wanted to do it like this." She drew his cock out and stroked his length. The soft skin of her hand felt incredible.

Far be it from him to deny her a fantasy. Fuck, this *was a* dream come true, and he hadn't even realized it. When she closed the wet heat of her mouth over his dick, he forgot where he was. Nothing mattered but the way she licked, kissed, and sucked him down her throat.

His hips bucked in his chair, but her hands on his thighs stilled him. She moaned softly around his cock; the vibrations going straight to his balls. Oh God, he was getting a blow job at work and anyone could hear them! Spots clouded his vision, his thighs quivered. Then he was coming and coming and coming. Nonstop down her throat, the only sound he dared make a whimper, as she swallowed everything he gave her and licked those thick lips.

She tucked him away and put him back to rights as he tried to remember his name. Work? Work who? He drew Jade into his lap and pulled her down for a kiss. "You minx. When I recover, I'm flipping that skirt up and fucking you over this desk."

Jade shook her head. "That was all for you, sugar."

"You're reckless."

"And you need to relax." She teased him, but she didn't leave his lap. It had become a joke between them, that he was too uptight and she was going to loosen him up. Which had led to some very interesting bedroom play.

He wasn't complaining. But he couldn't have done that if he'd had a meeting or a call.

"We're the only ones in the office?"

Jade nodded. "Upstairs anyway. Someone could have come from the club area."

Andrew's eyes popped wide in fear, but the thought was oddly arousing as well. He tamped that down. Once his mind cleared, his instincts told him to forbid it from ever happening again.

Yet, the building was silent. Andrew listed the occupants in his head according to the time. Mom wasn't there today, Aiden wouldn't be in yet, and no one else had any reason to come up to talk to him now that Jade had squared away their day-to-day business. He could... afford to be naughty?

Her hand on his face brought him back from his musings. "You still with me?"

"Yeah, sorry. I was just..."

"You were overthinking." She pressed a kiss to his cheek. "I made sure no one else was up here. Don't you trust me?"

Fuck. "Of course I do."

She slid his tie through her hands, a flirty grin on her face. Then she dropped a bomb. "So you won't argue about me taking the bus anymore?"

This again? "Baby, I can drive you. It has nothing to do with trust."

Jade sighed and rose from his lap. "I can't keep leaning on you like this."

"But the attacker—"

"Hasn't been seen or heard from in weeks."

"That we know of." She towered over him now, and he didn't like it. He stood up to even the playing field. "It's getting dark earlier these days. The bus isn't safe."

"Aiden has the security team on it, as well as the new camera."

" I have to make sure you're safe!"

"I can take care of myself!" She huffed and scrunched up her face. There was a moment of silence, and then her face relaxed, almost deliberately. "I was doing fine before you showed up. I don't need to be some kept woman."

Before he could say another word, Jade slammed his office door shut. He blinked and fell back into his chair in a daze from the emotional whiplash. What the fuck?

He groaned and laid his head on his desk. This reminded him of the one time he'd gotten involved with a coworker at the bank. Technically, they hadn't been employed yet; Rowan and Andrew had both been interns in their last semester of college. So the company fraternization rules hadn't applied to two horny twenty-one-year-olds. But Rowan hadn't been interested in him in a romantic sense. He used sex to distract Andrew from their assignments, letting Rowan take all the credit. The result was not only the loss of the position they had been competing for, but also of what he thought had been a potential romantic relationship.

Andrew thought Jade a better person than that. Had he really been so overbearing about the bus thing that she thought it necessary to *seduce* him into relenting? That attacker still hadn't been caught, and he doubted the police were taking it all that seriously, since the victims were queer. Her safety was at stake!

Jade fumed all the way to her desk. Her bus pass was expiring, and she had barely gotten her money's worth. The worst thing was how she caught herself expecting him to chauffeur her around now. Memaw would be ashamed. How had she let herself become dependent on a *guy*?

That had been a life lesson Memaw had drilled into her head. *Never give any man power over you, child,* she'd say.

They start out saying they only want to protect you, and that's when they get you. And she would know. Her husband controlled her and tried to make her quit her spirituality. The only reason Memaw had gotten away from him was her sisters and some family money that he couldn't access. But that controlling nature had been taught to his sons. Jade hated to think about her childhood and how it had shaped her, but the fact was that until she was sixteen, she had been stuck in a stifling environment thanks to her father and her assigned sex at birth.

After growing up under Leroy's belt, Ember's attacker wouldn't scare her. Jade *always* carried a can of pepper spray in her purse. She had contemplated trying to squeeze her baseball bat into a bag, but was worried it would hit someone by accident on public transportation.

She'd made Baltimore her home in college. Sure, it was partially out of financial necessity, but she'd built a family out of her friends. And Jade loved traveling by bus because she could watch the surrounding city. It grounded her in her home, where *she* chose to put down roots. Not because of some asinine blood connection, blood that didn't want her.

Now Andrew wanted to take her independence, that connection, away? Fuck that. She didn't need him.

Speak of the devil. Right then, he exited his office and made a beeline for her desk. Jade opened up the first program she saw to look busy.

"Did you seriously do that just to soften me up about the bus thing?" He fumed, spreading his hands on her desk and looming over her. "Were you using sex to manipulate me?"

Jade sighed. Good grief, one slip of the tongue and he had to make a mountain out of a molehill. "No, that wasn't the intent."

"I find that hard to believe."

"*Tough*." She'd enjoyed the power it gave her over him, albeit briefly. And she had been honest about it being a fantasy. The question about the bus had just blurted out of her mouth while her guard was down. And now the dream had been ruined forever.

But she wouldn't tell him that.

His face twisted in a snarl. "I don't appreciate being manipulated." Andrew crossed his arms over that fine muscular chest that Jade forced herself to ignore.

"I wasn't manipulating you! I just want to do things like a normal couple."

"Protecting you *is* normal!"

"I can protect myself!"

Andrew snorted. "Unbelievable."

"What's unbelievable is how much gas you're spending carting me around, when I have a perfectly good bus pass that's going to waste."

He threw his hands up in the air. "Okay, fine! You win."

Andrew stomped back to his office. But that wasn't the last she'd heard of it.

She should have known she would have her own personal bodyguard to the shelter on the corner. Andrew followed her out the door and down the block. That was the problem with guys who were tall like her. They could actually keep up with her stride. He even had the audacity to stand with her at the bus stop.

"What are you doing?"

"Making sure nothing happens."

Jade ground her molars as her eye twitched. Thankfully, the Maryland Transit Authority pulled up, the hydraulics squealing as it lowered down to the street level. As she took out her pass, she turned to glare at him. "No, you're smothering me. I want to be your girlfriend, not your ward, Mister Wayne."

She didn't look at him again as she boarded and found a seat.

The bus drove away as she buried her nose in her phone.

Jade: Do we have alcohol for girls' night?

Mia: Oh, I have booze. What do you want?

Jade: I need to get white-girl wasted.

Nadia: Holy fuck. :shocked emoji:

Rosie: What's wrong?

Before she could answer them, her cell rang in her trembling hand. She didn't recognize the number, but the area code belonged to New Orleans.

"Hello?"

"Hi, I'm looking for Jade Aguillard."

"This is she."

"Miss Aguillard, my name is Hilda. I was your grandmother's attorney."

A lawyer? Jade sat up straight in her seat and plugged her other ear with her finger so she wouldn't miss anything over the white noise of the bus.

Hilda continued. "Have any of Lou Ellen's children been in touch with you?"

"No, we're not on speaking terms."

She sighed, her tone apologetic. "I hate to be the one to tell you, but your grandmother passed away two days ago."

"What?" But they'd just spoken three days ago. And… fuck, she'd never called Memaw back.

Jade's skin tingled as she went numb with cold. Memaw… was dead.

Someone else must be inhabiting her body, because she had detached emotionally, despite giving Hilda her email so she could forward Jade some information. Apparently, she needed to be at the reading of the will. Her relatives had already taken possession of the body and arranged funerary rites for tomorrow.

As she hung up, she had the strangest sensation that this was happening to someone else. Not her.

She exited the bus in a daze and wandered towards Mia's apartment on the first floor. The door opened at her knock, and short, curvy Mia frowned up at her.

"Are you okay? You didn't answer Rosie in the chat."

"I... I got a phone call."

Mia pulled gently on her hand, and Jade stumbled inside. "You don't look so good, babe. What's going on?" After a minute of Jade sitting on her couch silently, Mia tried another tactic. "Who called?"

"Memaw's lawyer. I... I have to go to New Orleans."

"When?"

"As soon as possible." Jade's mask cracked as she verbalized what she was still processing. "Memaw... Memaw is dead. And Andrew and I..." She gasped for breath.

Pale arms wrapped around her in a tight embrace, holding her pieces together. "We got you, Jade. We're here to listen. Whenever you're ready, okay?"

Nadia slid onto the pink sofa and hugged her from the other side. "Let's start with Memaw?"

Jade took a deep breath, then blew it out. "I need help." God, that hurt to admit. But it was freeing all the same. She *couldn't* do everything on her own.

She managed to repeat what the lawyer told her as if on auto-pilot. Mia slipped into Jade's phone and found the details in her email. Then she was typing away.

"What are you doing?"

"Booking your flight and a hotel."

"But that's where I need help. I—I can't possibly afford it."

Mia didn't stop. "Nad, hand me my wallet."

Nadia retrieved her black and pink wallet with the Capricorn symbol. "What time does she need to be at the airport?"

"That depends on you, babe." Mia's brown eyes stared into hers. "Do you want to be there for the funeral?"

Jade shook her head. "No way. I have no desire to face *them*." She practically spat the last word. Her blood family hated her.

"Alright, so you can fly in Sunday and go to the reading Monday. I booked a three-day trip, but if you need more time, just call me, okay?" She nodded, and Mia wrapped her up in a hug. "Don't worry about the money. Order room service for whatever you want, they'll bill it to the room. I'm not taking no for an answer this time."

Jade nodded dumbly, her tears flowing fresh. She'd been blessed with the best friends a girl could ask for.

"What do you say we have a sleepover this weekend? It'll be just like old times when we had the dorm." Nadia rubbed circles into her back.

She wiped her wet cheeks. "But y'all have plans…"

"Cici has to work weekends. It's not a big deal."

"And Caleb is on the schedule tomorrow morning," Nadia said as her thumbs flew across her phone. She was probably checking in with her boyfriend as they spoke. "Why don't we run up to our floor and pack some bags, then we can order pizza and work on getting you white-girl wasted."

"Okay." Jade stood up and grabbed Nadia's out-stretched hand.

Mia stood from the couch, too. "I'm going to start on some margaritas. And then when everyone's here, you can tell us what happened with Andrew."

Jade groaned. "You caught that, didn't you?"

"Yup." Nadia opened Mia's door and waited for her. "I figure you only want to explain once if we can help it."

Chapter 13

Nadia: Okay, I made a separate group text cause y'all need to know what's happening.

Rosie: Is Jade okay?

Nadia: Not really. While she was texting us, she got a phone call from a lawyer. Memaw died. She showed up at Mia's crying.

Olivia: Oh no!

Rosie: Poor Jade. :crying emoji: I can't imagine losing Gram and Grandad.

Nadia: Mia's booked a flight and hotel for Sunday. I can take her to the airport, anyone who wants to tag along is welcome. And we're doing girls' night sleepover style tonight. I canceled my plans with Caleb for the weekend.

Rosie: I have work Saturday and Sunday, so I can't stay over.

Olivia: I'll let Jake know I can't watch his team play tomorrow. The kids will understand.

Mia: Apparently, something happened with Andrew as well.

Rosie: Dear God, give the girl a break!

Mia: Olivia, can you grab some ice cream or cookie dough? I gotta change my sheets.

Rosie: I made brownies for tonight. Also, gross. I don't want to know.

Olivia: Brownie sundaes it is. I'm packing a bag now and I'll stop on the way.

Mia: Perfect. See y'all when you get here.

———

Andrew didn't stick around the club after Jade's bus pulled away. He headed straight for his Explorer, bypassing the security guys at the door giving him the side-eye, and drove his grumpy ass home, stewing the entire way.

Where the hell had that all come from today? Things were going amazing. Or maybe that was just him. Maybe this had been bugging her for a while and she just hadn't said anything.

Lord, he was an idiot. That had to be what went wrong. He rubbed his temples, a headache coming on.

When he parked the car, the first thing he did before even turning it off was whip out his cell and text her.

Andrew: Did you make it home?

He was inside the apartment before his phone vibrated with a response, and Andrew remembered how much longer her commute was.

Jade: Yes, Bruce.

Okay, so she was still upset. She would be with her squad tonight, so Andrew figured it was best to let her be. But first he needed to apologize.

Andrew: I'm sorry I lost my head. Have fun tonight. Can I see you this weekend?

He waited, but nothing came through. Andrew figured she was already knee deep in girl-talk and didn't want to talk to him. That was fair. He'd been an ass, after all.

Now if only he could figure out why she was so insistent on taking the bus with danger lurking.

Andrew went through his usual nightly routine, changing into workout clothes and hitting the gym to work out his frustration. When he got back to his apartment ready for a shower, his twin nearly gave him a heart attack.

"What are you doing here?"

Aiden bent over and peered inside his fridge. "All you have in here is leftovers."

Andrew leaned against the counter and crossed his arms. "That doesn't answer my question."

"Well, hello to you, too, Brother."

He pinched the bridge of his nose and squeezed his eyes shut. The tension was back in his shoulders and he reeked of sweat. "Aiden… don't make me regret giving you a key."

"But we swapped keys in case of an emergency!"

"And how, exactly, is this an emergency?" Andrew wanted to wallow and his twin was in his way.

"Based on the state of your fridge, I think this qualifies as an intervention."

"What?"

"Go shower and get changed. Jeffrey has a show tonight and you're coming with me."

Andrew cocked an eyebrow. "Is it a dinner show?"

"No." Aiden smirked. "We're going to stop for that on the way."

"Alright." He could use this time to pick Aiden's brain about what the hell happened back in his office. "Let me shower and we'll go."

"Can you drive?" Aiden batted his eyelashes.

Andrew just snorted. "You want to drag me out *and* make me the DD, too? Maybe I'll just order in."

His twin pouted. "But —!"

He palmed his forehead and growled. "Look, I've had a hell of a day and if anyone deserves to drink tonight, it's me."

Aiden's brow folded. "What happened?"

Andrew sighed. "We're wasting time. I need to shower."

"Alright, I'll drive us if you tell me what's wrong."

"I'll tell you when there's a drink in my hand." He strode into the bathroom and tossed his workout clothes off. Then he started the water heating up. Tucking his dreadlocks into a shower cap, Andrew stepped under the warm spray and started scrubbing the funk from his skin.

"What are you wearing?" Aiden called from the hallway.

"Clothes," said Andrew.

Aiden poked his head into the bathroom. "That's not helpful. You need to look good to represent me and Jeffrey."

Andrew rolled his eyes. "I'm not the drag artist. No one's going to look at me."

"The queens will be."

"I have a girlfriend. I think." He muttered the last part under his breath.

Apparently not quiet enough. Aiden appeared and leaned against the doorjamb. "Are you and Jade okay?"

Andrew sighed as he turned off the water. "I don't know. She's mad at me for trying to protect her." He stepped out of the shower and toweled off, completely fine with being nude in front of his twin. They'd shared a womb, after all.

"What did you do?" Aiden sang as he fisted one hand on his hip.

"Why do you assume it was me?" Andrew's exasperated response came as he pulled off the shower cap and threw the towel over his rack to dry.

Except he knew he was at fault. He just didn't understand *why*.

"Because I know you." Aiden followed him into the bedroom and sat cross-legged on his bed.

Andrew pulled on his underwear, then reached into the closet and grabbed the first shirt his hand closed around. Damn. He'd picked the black dress shirt with the subtle satin pinstripes that he'd been wearing the night he met Jade.

Fuck it.

He dabbed on some cologne and threw the shirt on anyway, perhaps to punish himself. Andrew wanted the reminder that his heart belonged to Jade. Socks and jeans were next, then his shoes.

"Aren't you going to tell me?" Aiden sat patiently on the bed.

"I need alcohol to go over this." He checked his reflection in the mirror, then tied his locs back in a ponytail. "Where do you want to go?"

"I was going to let you pick."

Andrew just shook his head. "I don't care as long as there's whiskey."

Aiden slapped him on the shoulder. "This sounds bad. Okay Romeo, let's go."

His twin drove him to an Irish pub, then waited until he had a shot in his hand and they put their food order in.

"Alright, Bro. Spill."

Andrew threw the whiskey back and stifled his cough as it burned on the way down. Then he repeated the events of the afternoon, omitting the mind-blowing blowjob Jade had given him in his office. That wasn't any of Aiden's business.

"Doesn't she understand I'm just trying to protect her?" He held his head in his hands. "Aiden, I can't lose her."

Aiden rubbed a hand over his eyes. "Andrew... She's an independent woman and you're stepping on her toes. I understand where you're coming from," he threw up his hands when Andrew glared, "but you're coming off as controlling."

Andrew groaned and laid his head on the dark wood table. "What am I gonna do?"

"Let her cool off, then apologize, and back the fuck off about the bus thing. If you're not going to the same place after work, it doesn't make sense to keep insisting."

"I don't want that asshole to get a hold of her."

"Listen." Aiden leaned forward, serious as a funeral. "It's not like before. She's not a high school student."

Andrew sighed. The problem with talking to his twin about this was, Aiden knew all the skeletons in his closet. "Let's not talk about them."

Aiden nodded his understanding. "We're doing the best we can, you know that. Hopefully, he shows up on camera soon and we can put this to bed."

"I'll drink to that." Andrew clinked his water glass against Aiden's. His brother let him change the subject then, as Andrew asked about Jeffrey's show. But in the back of his mind, he wondered how to fix this *and* keep Jade from getting hurt.

* * *

Jade stuffed a change of clothes and her pajamas into the old weekender bag she'd found at the thrift store ages ago. Her toothbrush and toothpaste were next. Did she need her phone charger? How much battery did she even have left?

Twenty percent. And an unread text from Andrew.

Andrew: Did you make it home?

Ugh. Jade typed out her response and then threw her phone into the bag.

Jade: Yes, Bruce.

On second thought... She fished it back out along with the charger and plugged them into the wall. Jade needed to ignore her cell for a while. Her boyfriend was in the doghouse, and he knew where she'd be tonight.

He didn't need to worry about her.

Jade threw her bag over her shoulder, turned out all her lights, and locked the apartment door behind her. Down the hall, Nadia was waiting for her.

"Got everything you need?"

"Yup. Let's get this sleepover started." Jade followed her down the stairs back to Mia's apartment. Olivia stood there, knocking on the door.

"Jade!" She dropped her bags and wrapped her arms around Jade, who hugged her in return. "I'm so sorry about Memaw."

She blinked back tears. "Me, too."

"Was she sick?" Olivia pulled back, her bright blue eyes full of sympathy.

Wasn't that the million-dollar question? "I don't know. She'd been acting strange lately, but when I asked, she'd just tell me she was fine."

"Fine as in fine, or as in *fine*?" Nadia raised an eyebrow.

Jade just shrugged as Mia opened the door. "I guess I'll find out when I get there."

"I got vanilla and chocolate, as well as some fudge sauce, whipped cream, and sprinkles."

Whipped cream? "Is this a sleepover or an orgy?"

Mia snorted, then bent over laughing, holding her stomach. "We're making sundaes! You perv."

"Pretty sure Jake would want pictures if it was an orgy." Olivia rolled her eyes. "That man. I swear."

Mia shook her finger at Olivia. "Wait for the man problems until Rosie gets here with the brownies."

Now Jade understood what the accouterments were for. "Ooh scratch brownie sundaes? Y'all are too good to me."

Rosie arrived after her shift, all ready for bed, with brownies in tow. "I can't stay over. I have to cover a shift tomorrow," she said as she hugged Jade tight. "I'm so sorry about your grandma."

Jade held onto Rosie the tightest. She'd been raised by her grandparents too, so she understood first-hand how close Jade and Memaw had been.

"Strawberry margaritas are in the blender!" Mia called from the kitchen. "Olivia, did you order the pizza?"

"On it!" The other blonde was typing away at her phone. "I was gonna get a large Hawaiian. We all good with that?"

Jade grinned. Olivia's boyfriend liked to tease her that pineapple didn't belong on pizza, but no one else ever minded.

"Can I get a medium spinach and mushroom?" Rosie asked.

"Yup." Olivia dug into her purse for her card.

"How are we all sleeping in here, Mia?" Jade wondered aloud.

"There's room for two in my bed, and one on the couch..." Mia handed Jade a drink and tapped on her chin. "We could throw the couch cushions on the floor for two people?"

"Who sleeps at a sleepover, anyway?" Nadia pushed her black frame glasses up her nose.

"Good point."

"Yeah, I thought we were going to Mario Kart the night away. Okay, pizza should be here in thirty." Olivia put her phone down. "I'll set the tip money by the door, then let's get Jade drunk."

Oh right. She had to recount the fight she'd had with Andrew. Jade took a big slurp of her frozen beverage and nearly choked. "Mia! How much tequila did you put in here?"

Mia's purple-tipped tresses bounced as she shrugged. "All of it?"

"Lord have mercy." Jade took a much smaller sip this time. "Pace yourselves, girls."

The squad grabbed their beverages and gathered around the coffee table. "Now that we're all here, what happened with Andrew?" Nadia asked.

Jade cradled her forehead in her hands. "He's been driving me crazy with the bus thing. I carry pepper spray in my purse and I can defend myself. Not to mention it's usually still light out and the club isn't open when I leave work." She rubbed circles into her temples with her thumbs as the girls waited for her to continue. "We were talking in his office and he told me he trusted me. So then I blurted out, like an idiot, 'So you won't argue about me taking the bus anymore?' And then we argued, and he accused me of using sex to manipulate him."

"Hold up there, chica." Mia raised her hand. "How did you use sex to manipulate him?"

She rubbed the back of her neck and grimaced. "I went down on him in the office right before this."

They almost missed the buzz of the intercom over their hooting. Nadia was closest to the door, so she jumped up to let their delivery person in.

"That wasn't your intention, was it?" Rosie asked.

"No, of course not." Jade sighed.

"Did you tell him that?" Olivia came back to the table carrying plates and napkins.

Jade helped her pass them out. "I did, but he doesn't believe me."

Olivia snorted. "Why am I not surprised?"

"Just give him a couple of days to cool off and then talk to him." Nadia carried the boxes back to the table.

"Have you heard from him at all?" Rosie pulled her smaller box towards her and laid two slices on her plate.

"He texted me, asking if I got home safe." Jade held her plate out to Nadia, who put two piping hot pieces of pizza with ham, bacon, and pineapple on it. "I insisted on riding the bus. Which he stood and waited for with me." She rolled her eyes.

Rosie cooed. "That was sweet."

Jade shook her head. "And totally unnecessary."

"But he still cares. This isn't hopeless." Mia pointed out.

"And then on the bus, I got that call from Memaw's lawyer. Now I have to go to New Orleans in two days." Salt and sweetness exploded on her tongue as Jade bit into her food. "When it rains, it pours."

"It's really unfair of the universe to dump both of these on you at once." Nadia wiped her mouth with a napkin.

"Yeah. I just want to forget everything tonight."

"And that, my friend, is what we're doing." Mia clinked her glass with Jade's. "Everyone save room for sundaes and then it's Mario Kart time."

Chapter 14

W HEN J ADE FAILED TO show up to work on Monday, Andrew couldn't help but think the worst. He'd barely gotten any sleep that weekend, ruminating over their argument and his unanswered text. Aiden had been zero help. Tossing and turning with regret when he had finally realized the crux of the matter was faith. She'd felt that he didn't trust her. And after confirming that he did, he turned around and acted like an idiot.

He needed to grovel. Now she was missing, and he fought to keep his fears at bay. At least until he heard Monica walking into her office.

"Mom!" He rushed inside the room. She spun to face him, her eyebrows high on her forehead.

"Andrew? Is everything alright?"

"Where's Jade?"

His mother took off her jacket and set it on the coat tree in the corner. "She called off. She won't be in for a while."

"Is she okay? Did she get attacked?" Could this bastard have found her closer to home, or somewhere along the bus line?

Monica raised one eyebrow at his antics and leaned back in her chair. "I'm afraid I can't give you the details. She specifically asked me not to."

Shit. *Shit*. He'd fucked up. And he didn't know if she was okay.

"Mom, please. She took the MTA on Friday, and that guy's still out there."

Monica just shook her head. "You'll have to ask her."

This was getting him nowhere. She had that "you need to learn this lesson the hard way" look on her face that had played such a role in his adolescence. Resigned, he apologized and headed back to his office. Once the door shut behind him, his cell jumped into his hand and he dialed Jade's number.

It rang and rang. "Come on, baby, pick up," he muttered as he paced the carpet. But all he got was her voicemail. He tried texting.

Nothing. He called again at several points throughout the day, but she didn't pick up. Finally, he phoned a florist, ordered a dozen red carnations (apparently roses weren't in season in October) for pickup, and left work an hour early. He'd never be able to focus until he saw her with his own eyes.

A couple hours later, after fighting rush hour traffic, he stood outside her apartment building and buzzed her intercom. No answer. Buzzed her again. Silence. He rang a third time, and then the speaker clicked on, but it wasn't Jade who answered.

"Who are you and why are you buzzing apartment fourteen? She's not here."

That voice sounded familiar. Which of Jade's friends lived on her floor again?

"Nadia, it's Andrew. I need to talk to Jade. Please."

Voices murmured in the background. It seemed she had company. Jade? "We'll meet you downstairs." The door lock gave way, and Andrew hurried inside.

He gazed up the stairs with hope in his heart, only to have those hopes dashed when Nadia and Mia came down to greet him. They crossed their arms and glared at him, forming a wall between him and his beloved.

Andrew deserved no less.

"She told you then."

Nadia pushed her black glasses up her nose. "She told us enough. What do you want, Andrew?"

He switched the flowers to his other hand so his sweaty palm didn't drop them. "I wanted to apologize to Jade. I — I hurt her, and I feel terrible, and I need to fix this. But she called off work and isn't answering her phone. Have you seen her?"

Mia and Nadia looked at each other, having what appeared to be a telepathic conversation. Then Nadia gestured to the bouquet in his fist, and her voice dripped with disdain. "Carnations?"

He shrugged. "Apparently they can't get roses this time of year."

Great. Now his flowers didn't pass muster.

At the skeptical look the ladies gave him, he ran his free hand over the back of his neck. "It's the only Black queer-owned florist shop in the city. I thought she'd appreciate that."

Their shoulders dropped slightly when he shared that tidbit. But Mia shrugged. "It doesn't matter. They'll be dead by the time she gets home."

Andrew's mind raced once more. "Where did she go?"

Nadia pursed her lips. "Uh-uh, we can't tell you that. Not after what you said."

Frustration burned in his chest. "How can I fix it if she won't talk to me?" They didn't have an answer for that.

Andrew begged. "Please. I promise if you explain where she is, I will make this right. I'll do anything."

Mia tugged Nadia's hand, and the two walked off to the side. They whispered back and forth furiously. Andrew's stomach churned as he awaited his fate.

When they returned, Mia led the way. "I'll tell you where she is and why she left. But you have to earn the information."

Light blossomed in his chest for the first time since their argument. Jade was so desperately lucky to have friends like these, which he could appreciate even if they weren't on his side yet. "What do you need me to do?"

Nadia smirked as she pulled out her phone. "You have to beat Mia at *Halo*."

"*Halo*?" He thought that was a one-player game.

"Tournament style." Mia answered the question he didn't ask. "Most kills in three matches."

He eyed up the short lady gamer. "You've done this before."

Nadia grinned, but it wasn't friendly. "She won us lots of free pizza in college. You in?"

Andrew gulped. If these were their terms, he had no choice. It'd been ages since he'd played, but humiliation was a small price to pay for the chance to fix his mistake. Maybe he could convince them to take pity on him regardless of whether he won. Or maybe they'd say something and he could figure out what happened.

"Alright, I'm in."

"Jake's bringing his system over. We're going to set up a LAN." Nadia kept typing. "How do you feel about tuna casserole?"

"Uh, I guess it's okay?" Was this another weird test?

Mia rolled her eyes. "I need sustenance to mop the floor with you. And I won't make you play on an empty stomach." She looked over at Nadia. "I take it Jake cooked?"

"Yup," Nadia replied. "He offered to bring it over with him and Olivia."

Hunger would be the least of his worries. He was on their turf and about to play a game he hadn't played in a while. With the audience rooting for his competition.

"It's been years since I played Halo. Can I get a practice round?"

Mia shrugged. "Seems fair."

Jade had arrived early at the attorney's office, and she was thankful she had. Hilda Stewart, an older woman with graying hair and a kind smile, had shaken Jade's hand and let her move a chair apart from the others, so she wouldn't have to sit so close to her relatives. She didn't say anything outright, but from the understanding look on her face, it was clear Memaw had informed her that the rest of the family would not welcome Jade.

Coming back to Louisiana to face her clan was her own personal hell. The last time she saw them, her father had nearly beaten her and the only thing that saved her was Memaw stepping in. Her father's generation had accused her of bringing shame to them, and refused to use any name for her from then on. She'd be "it" to them forevermore.

But now, she was no longer a girl pretending to be a boy to make her father happy. Today she was clearly the woman she was meant to be. Would they even recognize her?

Did she want them to?

No, it would be easier if they didn't. Jade's nerves were raw; not only had she needed to ask favors from her friends to get here, she'd lost her anchors in this world.

Both of them. Because while Memaw had been her connection to the past, Andrew had felt like a tie to the future. Until the fight. But she would rather be alone for the rest of her life than live with a man who thought she was incapable. She needed a partner who would trust her, both in word and action.

It might have been the strange woman's presence in the office, but when her parents, aunts, uncles, sisters and their husbands arrived, they blessedly ignored her. A few cousins trailed in; at least that's who she assumed they were. Everybody had changed in the eight years since she had seen them.

"Everyone, thank you for coming today," Hilda began. "First, let me express my sincere condolences. Lou Ellen was a joy to have as a client, and I'm sorry for your loss."

Quick nods and a few murmured thanks hummed at Jade's back, her gaze fixed firmly on the closest thing she had to an ally in the room.

"Now, instead of simply reading the will, she asked me to play a video. There is a proper paper document as well, if anyone wants me to read that, but I believe this sums everything up nicely." She gestured to the small monitor on her desk, which was turned around to face the office.

Jade's lip quivered as she fought fresh tears. She didn't dare let these vultures catch her in a vulnerable state. Swallowing her nausea, Jade injected steel into her spine as she prepared to see her beloved grandmother for the first time in over two years.

The video started with Memaw sitting in this same office, in a chair very similar to the one Jade sat in now. It was like she was really there with them, and it freaked her out just a little.

"Are we recording?" Lou Ellen squinted at someone off camera, then looked back dead center. She hesitated for a moment. That was so unlike her. Jade took the few seconds to inhale everything she could see of her grandmother; she was even thinner than usual, her brown skin sallow. Her snow-white curls hid under a colorful scarf, but no one could have missed the dark circles under her eyes.

"Hello, everyone. If you're seeing this, you either hacked my lawyer's computer, or I've gone to be with the ancestors. They are calling me home, and I fear I must go soon. You see, the doctors have diagnosed me with stage four liver cancer, and there isn't much they can do." Memaw stopped to give them a sardonic chuckle. "You know it's bad if *I'm* going to a doctor."

Jade bit her lip. She'd *known* something was wrong when her grandmother slipped up in their phone call!

Why didn't you tell *me?*

"I kept quiet about the diagnosis, because I wanted to live my life to its natural conclusion. I didn't want a pity party, or a bunch of relatives coming to see me out of obligation, or some load of crap like that." Memaw adjusted her glasses. And Jade smiled despite her pain, because she knew school was in session.

She addressed each of her children by name, calling them out for taking their father's side in the split and other slights, some Jade had witnessed and some she hadn't. While Grandfather had refused to divorce her when he was alive, they'd separated long before Jade was born. He'd tried to make her quit her Voodoo practices, and she'd declined.

"And you, Leroy. You are the worst of all. While I still came around after what y'all did to me, to reject your own child is a sin on its own level. I will explain the mistakes I made raising mine, and you will answer for your own. But I did what I felt was right and at least I can say, I did something right with her."

She referred, of course, to Jade leaving Slidell and moving in with her in New Orleans.

"Despite the distance, Jade has remained a constant in my life. And that is why I, Louise Ellen Aguillard, being of sound mind and body, leave all my earthly possessions to my grand*daughter*, Jade Aguillard."

Hilda paused the video as Jade's entire blood family shouted in protest. They'd all wanted a piece of the big old house in New Orleans that she'd transitioned in. It was likely the only reason they had shown up at all. All Memaw's money, her value to them, was tied up in it. Jade smiled internally as she realized that was why Memaw hadn't told a soul about her illness; someone would have tried to talk her into signing it away.

Her relatives got up to go, obscenities on their tongues and hate in their eyes for her. Someone shouted about contesting the will when they were outside in the hall. When the room was empty besides her and the lawyer, she picked up her purse to leave as well.

"Don't take off yet, Jade." Hilda gave her a small smile. "She has more to say, but it's to you alone." She shook her head. "It's like she *knew* they wouldn't stay to hear the rest."

Jade chuckled even as a tear escaped her eye, and nodded. That was Memaw.

A box of tissues appeared before her face. Jade reached out to take them, and Hilda strode to the door and locked it. Then she pulled a chair over next to Jade's and sat down.

"Are you ready to continue?"

No. Never. "As ready as I'll ever be."

Hilda raised her hand and pushed a button on a small remote. Memaw's video started again.

"Jade, child, I know you don't want to stay here. So why would I leave you the house? Simple. It's all I have left. And none of my ungrateful kids are going to leave anything for you unless I do. You have spent far too long in this family without power, without a voice. So that is my gift to you."

Power? A voice? But Memaw had given her those years before when she took her in and applied for guardianship over her as a teen. She'd backed her at the high school, helped her get health insurance, supported her through the first stages of her transition and got her to college. All of Jade's power, her strength, came from the frail little woman on the screen.

"Do whatever you want with it. All of it. Take what you need back to Baltimore. *You* have the authority. Let them go through it, but only if you're feeling generous. If there was anything they wanted, they could have spent some damn time with me over the last eight years. Then rent it out for the income, or sell it! I don't care. I couldn't get you that surgery any other way, and that is my strongest regret that I leave this life with: not being able to fully fix your birth certificate."

Memaw leaned forward, and Jade blinked furiously to clear her vision.

"You're smart, baby, and I know you'll figure out how best to handle the house. Make your dreams come true, Jade. I'm so proud of you." Memaw winked. "I'll see you on the other side. Love you more."

Her breaths came fast and shallow as her stomach knotted. Tears that she had denied for days ran down both cheeks. The weight of Hilda's arm around her shoulders as she sobbed into the tissues in her hands eventually brought her back to the present.

Disgusted that she'd broken down in front of a complete stranger, Jade's face heated. "I'm so sorry. I was apparently the last to hear she was gone, despite our weekly phone calls."

Hilda patted her on the back and withdrew her arm. "It's alright. I'm sorry I was the one that had to make that call. By the time I found out, the family had made their arrangements." Jade nodded. Memaw hadn't wanted a Catholic burial, but of course her father and aunts and uncles wouldn't care.

Hilda stood and went to her desk, motioning her forward. Jade signed the paperwork Hilda sat in front of her, that she had read the will and received the property. She glanced sideways at the monitor. "Can I get a copy of that video? I haven't seen her in so long..."

The attorney smiled and withdrew the thumb drive that Jade only now noticed was sticking out of her computer tower. Hilda then showed her the key in the manila envelope with her official printout of the will, slid everything inside, and handed the whole pile to Jade.

Jade's brows furrowed, wishing she could talk to someone about a new funeral for Memaw. A proper Voodoo ceremony, if there was such a thing. "Has anyone told her friends? They would want to say goodbye in their own way."

"She mentioned a shop that she frequented. The address is inside. She seemed close to the owner, Patience Manuel."

Jade nodded. "Thank you for... everything." It had been a lot easier to deal with her family with the lawyer present.

"My pleasure. Take care, Jade."

"You, too."

Jade stepped out onto the street, the harsh sunlight preying on her weary eyes. All around her, pedestrians crawled the streets of downtown New Orleans, going about their business like her world hadn't come to a screeching halt. She wandered down Loyola Avenue back towards her room, a salmon swimming upstream, a stranger in a strange land. Mia spent way too much money on her and put her up in a fancy hotel only a few blocks from the lawyer's office, but Jade now had a house. She didn't know what state it would be in, but she needed to see it. Memaw's Voodoo community should have been notified yesterday. And her rental car, that Mia had also paid for, was in the hotel garage.

But first, she had to get out of her heels.

Hugging the envelope to her stomach, she passed through the lobby, ignoring the businessmen loitering and discussing nothing, as well as the glittering waterfall chandelier hanging from the ceiling two stories up. Her shoes clicked against the polished stone floor. She had tunnel vision for the elevators.

Get in. Change clothes. Find Patience. Go to the house.

So when a hand landed on her shoulder, she gasped and jumped a mile, terrified one of her relatives had found her. But when she turned, her heart beat fast for a completely different reason.

"Andrew? What are you doing here?"

Chapter 15

His Oxford shirt was wrinkled, his collar undone. She watched his Adam's apple bob as he gulped.

"Jade, baby, I am so sorry."

She was a woman on a mission, and she did not have the energy to deal with anything else. "Answer me." He jolted at her tone. "Please," she added, a weak and desperate attempt to soothe the wound she'd inflicted.

He grabbed the back of his neck. "I'm sorry, I just — I didn't know where you were, Mom wouldn't give me any information, and I needed... I wanted to fix things between us."

"Andrew..." Jade sighed. If this were one of Mia's movies, the screenwriter would write this as a highly romantic grand gesture. But she didn't have the energy to act. "I'm dealing with a lot right now. I wasn't expecting to see you until I got back." Had his mother ratted her out? "How did you know where I was?"

"Mia told me."

What the hell? That meddling matchmaker!

"Before you get mad, she said to tell you I beat her in *Halo* fair and square. She promised if I could do that, she'd explain where you were."

Halo? Andrew had beaten *Mia* in *Halo*?

"I... I had to find you."

Jade opened up her phone to tell her friend she was in the doghouse, but there was a text waiting for her.

> Mia: I'm sorry. He's really cute when he begs. And he will probably be even cuter when it's you. Make him work for it. I sure as hell did.

Jade exhaled sharply and shook her head. At least Mia was ultimately still on Team Jade. She'd never go easy on an opponent.

"Look," she started as she slid her phone back into her purse, "my grandmother is dead and I inherited everything and now I have to deal with it. I'm not sure when I can return to work. I'll need to figure out what to do with her home, the furniture, all of it. I don't know what I want or what's in good enough condition to take home with me." And she had no idea how much shipping it would cost. "I'm heading upstairs to get changed and then I'm going to the house. If you want to talk, you'll have to come with me."

⸺ℓℓℓ ⸺

Even cold and aloof, with red-rimmed eyes and puffy cheeks, Jade was a beautiful sight for Andrew's sore gaze. But something about her speech bothered him.

She thought he was here about *work*?

The Neon Unicorn could burn down for all he cared right now. What mattered was fixing things with Jade.

Who was stepping on the elevator and about to get away again.

Andrew shook out of his musings and ran inside after her just as the doors started to slide shut. He stood as close to her as he dared without touching. Watching her face, he tried to form the perfect words to say to her, but instead he prayed for a sign there was any hope for them. He got one when the elevator chimed on her floor, and she glanced at him from the side. There was confusion, but also desire in her warm brown eyes.

He *couldn't* fuck this up again.

She slowed her pace to a normal walk as they traveled down the hall, still clutching that envelope to her stomach like a life vest. Pulling a keycard from her purse, she hesitated in front of a door.

"Are you coming in?"

"I didn't think you'd want to have this conversation out here," he murmured. When she pursed her lips, he put his hands up, promising to keep them off her. "I just want to talk, baby."

"Okay."

He followed her into a small suite, where she disappeared behind a partial wall into a room with a neat bed. With his back to the semi-private bedroom, he took a seat on the sectional couch next to her windows overlooking downtown.

"I didn't mean to smother you, Jade." His heart thudded in his chest as he listened to her unzip her suitcase and the rustle of fabric. "I never wanted to make you think I questioned your intelligence. You're incredible, and I've... I've seen some ugly shit happen. I really just wanted to protect you."

"You think I *haven't*?" She challenged him from the other room. "I was in an entire room *full* of ugly this morning. And I didn't need protection."

Andrew swore someone had a vise wrapped around his heart and was twisting it. She shouldn't have had to face her estranged, unsupportive family alone. He fought down the taste of failure and closed his eyes.

"Can I tell you a story? I think it will help explain things." He held his breath while he waited for her reply.

Her sigh rang from the bedroom. "I have a little time."

"Thank you." Exhaling, he unclenched his fists and leaned his head against the couch, prepared to bare his soul. "When Aiden and I were fifteen, his job transferred my dad to Baltimore for work. We ended up in one of the rougher schools at the time; they closed it not long after I graduated. No one knew what to do with a couple of biracial boys from northern Virginia; that's why Aiden and I are so close. We had to rely on each other; too white for the Black kids and too Black for the white kids... except for River."

Andrew threw another card down on the wooden surface and turned his land to the side. He and Aiden were playing Magic the Gathering *at the same table in the corner like they did every lunch period. No one else spoke to them outside of whatever was necessary in class. So that's why when a tray appeared out of the corner of his eye, Andrew's guard went up.*

"Mind if I sit here?"

He turned and stared into the bluest gaze he'd ever seen. Short blonde hair flopped over a friendly, light-skinned face. Andrew looked at Aiden, who shrugged and played another card. The kid sat down and introduced themselves as River, adding, "My pronouns are they/them." It was the first time Andrew had heard the phrase.

The three became fast friends, eating lunch collectively every day and walking home together after school. Next to his twin, River grew into his best friend. He didn't remember anymore what happened, but by Christmas he had a crush on the kid. One wintry afternoon, their friend was telling a story and not paying attention, and almost walked across the street as a truck was driving by. Reaching out, Andrew grabbed them by the hand and pulled them to safety. River's face turned pink when they looked back at him, and from then on they traveled hand-in-hand, Aiden leading a few feet ahead. It took him until Valentine's Day to confess his feelings, after constant nagging from his brother.

Theirs had been an innocent puppy love, with soft kisses and movie-time cuddles. It made him realize he was attracted to hearts, not parts. He didn't adopt the label pansexual until he was an adult, but in hindsight, that's what fit him.

People at school took notice. Outcasts that banded together were dangerous to the status quo. One day, some football players started a fight with him in gym class. Aiden jumped in as well, of course, and all of them received detention.

When they got home that evening, Andrew tried to get in touch with River. But no one picked up at their house. This was the early days of cell phones, and they were expensive and bulky. Few people owned them.

He had to leave a message on the answering machine, asking River to call him back. Late that night, as he was getting ready for bed, his mother came to his bedroom door.

"Andrew, River's mom just called. They were attacked on the way home today, and they're in the hospital."

He clutched his arms around his chest and tried to swallow the sour taste from his mouth. "Did their mom say what happened?"

His beautiful ginger-haired mother, with her laughing Irish eyes, seemed to age ten years that night. "She doesn't know. They haven't regained consciousness yet."

A whimper escaped his throat and then Mom was hugging him, rocking him back and forth on the bed while he babbled and bawled. It was his fault; he hadn't been there to protect them.

The next day, she took the twins to see River. Andrew entered the room first with a fistful of flowers from the gift shop, while Aiden and Monica stood in the hallway to give them some privacy. River was unrecognizable, their shining face swollen and marred with purple bruises. Blood stained their fair hair near where a bandage had been wrapped around a head wound. Wires and tubes hooked them up to monitors.

Setting the vase on the tray table, Andrew gently picked up their hand. It had the least damage that he could see; a few scabbed-over scratches, but the usually neatly filed nails were ragged and torn.

"River?" He choked out as Aiden came to stand behind him and laid his hand on his shoulder.

Eyelashes fluttered and they turned their head to look in his direction. One purple eye had swollen shut, but the other squinted open. "Andrew? Where…"

He waited as his sweetheart woke up. Their brows furrowed in a foggy glare. As he opened his mouth, River finished their question.

"… were you?"

Startled, Andrew didn't speak right away. River groaned in pain and pulled their hand from his.

"I… I needed you! Where were you?" Alarms went off as their heart rate rose and nurses ran into the room in a flurry of activity. They ushered his family out into the hall, and he slumped against the wall.

"I want to go home," he'd said to his mother.

"Honey, this wasn't your fault."

But his heart lay shattered on the floor at River's bedside. "They don't want to see me."

Andrew hadn't noticed the tears dripping off his chin until gentle, long thumbs wiped his cheeks. At last, he opened his eyes to see Jade standing over him, an unreadable expression on her face.

"What happened then?"

Andrew sighed. "Their parents pulled them out of school. After they healed, the family moved away. I never spoke to them after that day. Our moms talked on the phone almost daily until the move, so I got updates. They pointed the finger at some other football players; it had been a coordinated attack to separate us so they could get at River."

"Did they press charges?"

His heart was breaking all over again. "They tried. But one kid's dad was a cop, so..." Andrew shrugged and made a 'what can you do?' gesture with his hands. "Nothing stuck."

Chapter 16

JADE SAT DOWN ON the corner of the tan sectional, the silence hanging heavily between them. Her heart broke for Andrew. His story explained so much; his reaction to Ember's transphobic attacker, and his protective nature. She felt compelled to explain why it chafed her.

"I was what some people call a 'change of life' baby. My parents thought they were done having kids, with three daughters in their teens. They named me Leroy, Jr. My father assumed I was his dream come true."

She huffed a sarcastic laugh, and Andrew put his palm on her arm. "Jade, you don't have to."

"I want to," she replied, then held his hand with her opposite one. She'd keep it brief. "The older I got, the less like him I turned out to be, despite his best attempts. I found my sisters' dress up chest in the attic long after they outgrew playing with it and came down the stairs dressed to the nines. That was the first time he used his belt to discipline me.

"I had no interest in sports, or working in construction like him. But I loved comics, specifically *X-Men*. I lied and told everyone Wolverine was the best character when it was really a toss-up between Storm and Rogue.

"He took me to a gamers' convention once, where we played these old-school games all afternoon. His favorite was *Mortal Kombat II*. I liked it too, especially the hidden ninja, Jade. I begged for a Nintendo and a copy of the most recent game for Christmas that year."

That day remained as the highlight of her childhood, and the time she'd felt the closest to her father.

"Eventually, I figured out who I really was. And I took the name Jade, not only because I admired the character, and how she emerged from the shadows, but also because I — I had some strange hope that my father would recognize the reference to his favorite video game."

She blinked back a tear, surprised she had any left after her earlier outburst. "It didn't save me from being kicked out when I came out of the closet. Memaw basically said to my parents, "I told you so," and took me home with her. After that, we only had each other."

Andrew squeezed her hand. "She knew?"

Jade chuckled sadly, remembering how her grandmother used to explain it to her. "Memaw was a Voodooist, and a good bit psychic. She swore up and down while my mother was pregnant with me that the baby would be another girl. It took me sixteen years to tell them she was right." She trembled. "And now, she's... gone. She was my best friend and my biggest ally for so long, and I'll never get to see her again."

She doubled over sobbing, but Andrew's arms held her up. He murmured apologies and condolences in her ear as he rubbed her back.

"She had cancer, and she didn't tell me. She should have told me!"

"Maybe she was worried that you would rush home when you just started a new job."

In fact, that's exactly what she would have done.

She leaned against him, her energy drained. "Those assholes wouldn't even give her the burial she preferred. I'm worried her soul won't rest without a Voodoo funeral rite."

"Can you talk to someone?"

Jade nodded against his shoulder. When had she wrapped her arms around him? It felt too good to back away now. "Her lawyer gave me an address and a name. I was going to head there, too."

"Could I go with you?"

He wanted to visit an occult shop with her? Jade sat up and looked at him, confused. "You want to?"

Cradling her face in his large hands, Andrew's gray gaze made her feel like something precious. "You don't have to do this alone. Please, all I've wanted was to help you. But I need to do better at expressing that. Let me prove I will stand beside you. We can take care of each other."

Jade searched her heart. They formed quite a pair, two tear-stained faces and grieving, broken hearts. But maybe, just maybe, they could fit their damaged pieces together and make a new whole.

"Okay." His hands still cupped her face, his gaze searching hers. She was close enough to count his freckles.

"I've missed you so much, baby." His eyes now focused on her mouth. Tired of words, Jade tilted her head and kissed him soundly on those plump pink lips.

Just as quickly, he held her to him, moaning and taking over the kiss. And she let him. She needed to relinquish control, if only for a moment. Being disciplined all the time was fucking exhausting. His tongue slipped into her mouth, gently tasting every crevice, memorizing it. Nothing else existed outside of the two of them.

After an eternity, he pulled back, and Jade slowly opened her eyes. The love shining out at her shocked her to her core. And the crazy thing was, she knew she loved him back. She didn't need the words. Then she glanced down and saw the smear of makeup on his shoulder.

"Crap, I smudged eyeshadow on your shirt." She tried to brush it away, much to his amusement. But it wouldn't come off. "Do you want to change?"

He shook his head. "I didn't bring any luggage."

"What? You mean you just hopped on a plane to New Orleans with no bags? No toiletries?"

Andrew shrugged. "Yep. I got the information from Mia and drove straight for the airport and asked for the next flight to NOLA."

Jade's jaw dropped. "But that's so expensive!" Who was this reckless man and what had he done with Andrew?

He smiled then and tucked a braid behind her ear. "Worth every penny."

Oh damn, he was good. If he hadn't won her over already, that would have done it. "What do you want to do about clothes?"

"I can grab a shirt from the shop downstairs. And there are always toothbrushes at hotel desks."

She shook her head. "How did you get here from the airport?"

"Taxi."

Thank goodness Mia had rented her a car. "My rental's parked in the garage. The gift shop's on the way."

He rose and offered her his hand. "Are you up to driving?"

"I think so." Jade stammered as she stood. He wasn't assuming he'd drive her, he was letting her call the shots. Andrew had *listened*. Her heart felt a million pounds lighter, probably because she had someone else to carry it now. She could do anything with this man at her side.

<hr>

Jade filled Andrew in on what had happened in the lawyer's office while she drove to Voodoo Mystique, the shop her grandmother had frequented. It sat on the edge of the French Quarter, a small sign in the window of a brown brick building that also housed a bar, an eye doctor's place, and a lingerie boutique. He grabbed her hand as they walked up the sidewalk to the red-trimmed door between two plate-glass windows. She looked back at him nervously, and he squeezed her palm to reassure her. He opened the door for her, and she entered as a bell chimed above their heads.

He let the door shut, and they both gawked. Scarlet walls peeked out behind masks and tapestries and shelves of goods. Jars of herbs stood proudly with chalkboard labels and colorful dolls sat around tables. Images of saints abounded. Andrew wasn't sure what he'd been expecting, but it was definitely not this.

"I'll be right wit' ya!" a voice called out. Jade released his hand and wandered toward the counter along the side of the shop. He followed.

A beaded curtain at the back wall parted, and a woman emerged. Her terra-cotta skin glowed against her bright caftan and head wrap, and when she smiled, her teeth showed a gap. He was unsure how old she was, but if she was a friend of Jade's Memaw, he'd have thought her to be older.

"How can I help ya fine folks?"

Jade walked up to the counter. "I'm looking for Patience Manuel."

The shopkeeper threw her arms wide. "You've found her!"

His darling hesitated, and Andrew stepped to her side. She needed to do this, but he could give her strength.

"M-my name is Jade. I'm... Lou Ellen's granddaughter."

Patience gasped, her eyes teary. "You're Jade? Oh, Lou Ellen will be so happy!" She came around the counter, grasping both of Jade's hands in her own. "She's missed you."

"I — I didn't get to see her. She never told me..."

A tilt of the head, and the shopkeeper understood. "Lou Ellen has gone to the spirit world?"

Jade nodded, tears coming once more. Andrew rubbed her back. God, she'd been through so fucking much, and it wasn't fair.

Patience noticed. "And this would be?"

He stuck his hand out to shake hers, but he noted she kept a hold of Jade's hands. "Andrew." Patience gave him a sly smile. He wasn't sure if he should assume the title of boyfriend or not, but it didn't seem to matter. She looked back at Jade.

"Lou Ellen said you'd met someone. She was over the moon, always talking about how proud she was of you."

Jade's expression darkened. "My — her children weren't respectful of her spirituality. Will she be okay with a Catholic ceremony?"

"Child, she's fine. We don't have a separate funeral rite. Most of us are practicing Catholics, anyway. And even if not, she knew what she was getting herself into with those kids." Patience patted her hands, and Jade seemed to breathe easier. Maybe her blood relatives hadn't fucked things up as much as she'd thought. Andrew was just grateful that the universe had gifted her with this peace of mind.

"I do have something of hers that you're going to want. Wait here." She disappeared behind the swinging beaded curtain once more, and Andrew wrapped an arm around Jade's shoulders.

"How are you holding up?"

She leaned her head on his shoulder and closed her eyes. "I feel better. She seems really nice."

"Yeah, she does."

The shopkeeper reappeared and handed Jade a square remote.

"Her garage door opener. I often brought her groceries after they confined her to the house."

Jade held the ancient-looking piece of plastic for a moment, then slipped it into her purse. "Thank you so much for watching out for her, and for being her friend."

"Aw, come here." Patience enveloped Jade in a hug. "Do see me if you ever return, Jade."

"Sure." Jade nodded. Just then, Andrew's stomach let out an embarrassing growl. Patience snorted.

"I think I better feed you." Jade took his hand once more. "Take care, Patience."

"You too." Patience waved as they left the shop. "Au re'oir!"

On the sidewalk once more, she tugged him back the way they came.

"Didn't you eat lunch?"

"Only if you count the peanuts on the airplane. Tell me where's good, I'll buy."

She slipped her arm around his and snuggled into his side. "Since you're here, you need an authentic New Orleans po'boy. I know just the place."

"Sounds amazing."

She took him to a seafood restaurant several blocks away with a sign declaring it the Gator Grill. They were seated in a courtyard with blue clapboard walls under an umbrella in the Louisiana sunshine. He poured over the menu, but everything sounded so good, he had no idea what to get.

Jade seemed a little more like her normal self. "You're in for a treat, sugar."

"I'm sure." A shiver tickled his spine when she called him "sugar." God, he'd missed that sexy-ass drawl. He studied Jade as she read over the offerings. "I can't possibly decide. Why don't you order for me, babe?"

She looked up from her menu in surprise. "You want me to?"

He shrugged. "You said I need an authentic po'boy, and you're the native around here."

Her small, pleased smile told him he'd done the right thing. "Do you prefer blackened or fried?"

"Whatever you think is better."

When the server arrived, she ordered them both the blackened catfish sandwich, which came to their table piled with lettuce, tomatoes, and onions, along with fries and coleslaw on the side. The planks of fish were perfectly seasoned and dressed with a zesty sauce on thick French bread. He'd never had anything like it.

The noises he made could have been embarrassing, but the courtyard was empty. They'd missed the lunch rush.

After they stuffed their faces, Andrew leaned across the space and looked Jade in the eye. "Ready for phase two?"

She huffed a laugh and smiled sadly at him. "Never."

"I would love to see where you grew up. It's yours now, after all."

Reaching over the table, Jade took his hand again. "Thank you. For everything. For coming out here and finding me and just... being here."

He lifted her palm to his lips and pressed a kiss to the inside of her wrist. "There's nowhere else I'd rather be."

<hr>

Oak trees dripping with Spanish moss stood sentry over Memaw's neighborhood. The house had been in her family for generations, and when she left Grandpa, she came back here because, "I knew he couldn't get his hands on it." Her sister had lived here, but she'd either moved out or passed on before Jade was born. While Memaw hadn't had much to live off, her home was paid for and, hopefully, in decent repair.

Jade had been pondering what to do with it all day. Memaw had suggested she rent it out or sell it, and use the money for her bottom surgery. But... Jade wasn't sure if she wanted to get GRS anymore. And she definitely didn't want to be a landlord.

Just thinking about selling the only house she'd ever been accepted in pained her heart. But she couldn't stay here. Her home was in Baltimore. The squad was there. Her job was there. And... Andrew was there.

As the SUV pulled up into the familiar ancient driveway, she reached for his hand, and he met her over the gearshift. She dug the opener out of her purse and hit the button to raise the door on the gray cinder block garage. On the left side, right where she'd last seen it, was Memaw's antique Oldsmobile sedan.

"She had a car?"

Jade nodded. "That's the same one she taught me to drive on. God, that brings back memories." The other bay was empty, and she carefully pulled in. Memaw's sister had added the building in more modern times, placing it right against the kitchen door so she didn't have to carry groceries outside in the rain. Thankfully, it was tall enough for the rental.

No sooner had they exited the vehicle than Andrew walked back out of the garage and gaped at the house. She smiled. The old 1860s second empire home was normal to her, but he'd probably never seen one quite like this before. He startled when she grabbed his hand and shut the door again. "Come on. I'll take you in the front so you get the full experience."

As she led him up the steps, she tried to see it from his perspective: an iconic sloping roof, red brick and regal white columns. But she also saw some shingles askew, probably damaged in a storm. Paint peeled off Memaw's beloved pillars and sage green shutters. And the iron railing across the porch had rusted.

How long had her grandmother been sick?

The porcelain doorknob nearly came off in her hand. Strengthened by Andrew's presence, she returned to what she considered her childhood home.

Inside, the house was dark, no light coming from the dusty chandelier above the foyer. When she flipped the switch, she found the heirloom furniture in the living area covered with sheets, probably done when Memaw realized she wasn't up to using the space anymore. Jade muscled the pocket doors to the dining room open, despite their protests, and spied the same dining table Memaw had when she'd been here. It hadn't been used much then, either.

"Damn, they must have had some big parties here back in the day." Andrew followed her inside and peered into the china cabinet. "Look at these dishes."

"Great-great-grandma did throw some fancy dinners in her time. That was all hers. It was passed down through her children and came to Memaw in the end."

"And now it's yours."

Yes, it was hers. She stared at the cut crystal goblets she hadn't once used. "What would I do with it?"

"Whatever you want."

She *should* let the aunts and uncles, cousins, and her father come through and take whatever they wanted. It was far too much for her to handle. Maybe Hilda would help her make the arrangements so she wouldn't have to deal with them directly. The next room she saw was the kitchen, which was spotless. Still dated back to the nineties when Memaw had last updated it, but the appliances were the same ones she'd bought when Jade was in high school. They should work fine. The refrigerator hummed and the lights all worked, so the electricity was paid up. She'd have to change all of that into her name until the house sold, and cover the bills herself. Ugh. Jade realized she might be in a bit over her head.

"The bedroom's small, but it's not bad," Andrew called from another doorway.

"Bedroom? There's no bedroom on this floor..." All four of them were upstairs. She marched over to where he stood, in the doorway to the den.

And when she found it, her heart broke all over again. A hospital bed had taken the place of Great-Grandpa's antique roll-up desk, a tall metal IV pole in the corner. The television had been angled so it could be seen from the bed, and Memaw's dresser was haphazardly squeezed into the tiny room. She'd confined herself to the first floor during her decline.

"This is... was... the den." Her voice trembled, and Andrew pulled her into his embrace, turning her so they walked right back out. He shut the door behind them and rubbed up and down her arms.

"Should we check for expired food?"

"Not a bad idea." Focusing on this new project, the two of them systematically went through Memaw's cupboards, checking the dates on all the packages. Andrew took the fridge. A few items got tossed into the garbage can. But what little was in the cabinets was still good.

"There's some fresh chicken in the fridge. Patience must have put it there not too long ago. What do you want to do with it?"

Jade shrugged. "I'm not hungry."

Andrew nodded. "Neither am I. That sandwich was huge. But we could cook it tomorrow if the gas is still on."

"We might as well." Memaw would want it that way. She hated food waste. God, what she wouldn't give to have some of her grandmother's cooking again. It had been ages since Memaw had cooked for her, and she was homesick for it.

Wait. Her recipe book! Jade had to have it. Even if she couldn't cook for her directly anymore, making her recipes would be the next best thing. She threw open the last cupboard on the right and there it was, the same tattered gray binder that she remembered. Tenderly, she pried it out of its home and hugged it to her chest.

"What's that?"

"Memaw's cookbook! I'm definitely taking this." This would be easy to take back to Baltimore on the plane.

"Does she have a chicken recipe in there?" He chuckled.

Memories hit her full force, and Jade groaned. "She made the best chicken in a spicy cream sauce that you've ever eaten." Laying the binder on the counter, she flipped through the pages until she found it. Written in Memaw's curly handwriting, the book detailed the secrets from one of Jade's favorite dishes. She felt like she'd inherited an ancient grimoire full of magic potions.

"I think there's everything but the cream here."

"We can get some on the way back tomorrow."

Andrew pressed a kiss to her temple. "You wanna show me your room?" He waggled his eyebrows, and Jade laughed.

"I believe she turned it into a library when I moved to Baltimore. But sure."

Holding the precious binder like a teddy bear, Jade led him up the dark wood steps to the second floor. A thick layer of dust coated everything up here. Opening the door to her old room, she stepped inside Memaw's library.

"Nothing left. But it's a wonderful feature."

"The ceilings in this house are so high." Andrew turned in a circle, looking at the bookshelves lining the wall. A padded armchair stood against one wall under a lamp, with a crocheted afghan laid across the arm like Memaw had just stepped away to answer the phone.

"They built it long before air conditioning."

He bent over to pick up a book on the side table, sweeping dust off it with his hand. "What the hell was your grandma reading?"

"She read a bit of everything. Why?"

"There's four shirtless guys on this cover."

What? Jade took the novel from him and turned it over. "Memaw was always a bit unorthodox, but I'd rather not think about her reading this." It was true. Memaw had given Jade the safe sex talk, not her father. And Memaw also made a point to understand how Jade's hormone treatments would affect her sexually. *Ain't nothing shameful about pleasure, child. You should know how your body works, especially with these shots.* That's what she'd said when Jade had asked her to stop talking to the doctor about it as an embarrassed, transitioning teen.

She saw the wisdom of it now.

They went through every inch of the house. Jade's mind spun with the sheer volume of *stuff* she had inherited. Most of Memaw's everyday clothes were down in the den, but her antique four-poster bed was still made up like she was going to move back upstairs any time. The third bedroom had apparently become storage when Memaw got too sick to take things into the attic.

Stars twinkled in the sky by the time they were done, and the sheer exhaustion of the day caught up to her. Jade flopped backward onto the queen-size mattress Memaw hadn't slept on in God knew how long, and sighed.

"I have no fucking idea what to do with it all."

Andrew lay next to her, his phone in his hand. "Well, one option, according to Google, is an estate sale."

The idea of strangers coming through and pricing out her heirlooms gave Jade the creeps. She thought of Great-great Grandma's good china and the crystal goblets. Things the previous generation remembered using, and had been planning to keep. And she couldn't take that from them.

Even if *they* wouldn't have left her a single crumb, she was no Grinch.

"I'll call Hilda in the morning and see if we could arrange for her kids to come through when I'm not here and just pick out whatever they want. All I need is Memaw's recipes. You can't put a price on those."

Andrew kissed her temple. "Then that's what we'll do. We can donate whatever's left, or… there's gotta be some antique shops around here."

Jade laughed. "Of course, sugar."

"Shall we go back to the hotel?"

She didn't answer right away as she took stock of herself. It had been such a long and emotional day. Jade felt like a wrung-out dishrag. Everything had been about Memaw, but she hadn't sensed her grandmother's presence anywhere but this room. And she was loath to leave it again.

"Could we sleep here? We can go back and get changed tomorrow, bring our stuff here. I just…" Jade's voice trailed off as she traced the designs sewn into the worn quilt.

Andrew propped himself up on his elbow and his kind eyes gazed down at her. "You wanna be close to her?"

She nodded.

"Whatever you want, baby."

Thank God he understood.

Chapter 17

Familiar laughter rang out as Jade made her way towards the front of the house. "Memaw?"

"I'm in here, child!"

The voices came from the living room. Bright sunlight shone through the windows, highlighting the vintage furniture in dark woods and rich red velvet, even more vibrant than Jade remembered them. Memaw, glowing in perfect health, sat on the settee. In the wingback chair, across the coffee table, was Andrew. They were both dressed up, sipping from Memaw's antique tea set that Jade swore had broken years ago.

"We going somewhere?"

"What, an old woman can't dress up for her guests?" Memaw tutted at her. "I was just having a lovely conversation with your young man here. It's about time you brought a boy home."

Jade went to sit in the other chair, but Andrew pulled her into his lap. She couldn't help but return his smile. "It's not my fault. It took me forever to find someone worthy of meeting you, Memaw."

Memaw beamed up at her.

Wait... this made no sense. "I don't understand. You were sick!"

"And now I'm all better!" Memaw threw her arms wide. "I told you everything was going to be alright, child."

"But... but the den! And the house!"

Her grandmother waited patiently as Jade sputtered. Then she rose from the couch and took Jade's face between her wrinkled hands.

"Jade, listen to me. I am fine. And I am so proud of you, and happy for you. I love you."

"Love you more, Memaw." Tears gathered in her eyes for their last goodbye.

She put a hand on each of their shoulders. "This has been fun. You two take care of each other now."

"Where are you going?"

Memaw shook her head. "I'm not the one leaving. But you need to go, and quickly."

Jade's brows furrowed, and she looked at Andrew, who seemed equally confused. "But we just got here."

"Jade, you're not supposed to *be* here." Worry struck Memaw's face, and she suddenly grew frantic as the room faded from sight. "Jade baby, wake up! You have to wake up!"

Wake up, *child!*

⌇

Glass crashed somewhere downstairs as Jade roused from her strange dream. She rubbed her eyes as she oriented herself. They were in Memaw's big fluffy queen bed in the house that was now hers.

"Call the cops, baby." Andrew tore the blanket away as he leaped to his feet and ran into the hall. Stopping a robbery in his underwear? Was he crazy?

Jade pulled her jeans up as she dialed the local emergency number she'd memorized as a teen. "What's your emergency?" the dispatcher answered.

"I think someone's breaking in!" Shouts rang out in the darkness. She rushed down the stairs as she rattled the address off to the operator.

"The police are on their way, ma'am. Please stay on the line."

She followed the noise to the kitchen. A shirtless Andrew wrestled on the floor with a masked intruder dressed in head-to-toe black. He overpowered them easily, but their small stature let them slip away. The two adversaries circled each other around the kitchen table.

Jade held her breath while each waited for the other to make their move. With their hands below the table, the small intruder slid something out of their hoodie pocket. A soft click, then the moonlight glinted off the edge of a barrel.

"Get down!" She leaped at Andrew and pushed him down just as the gun fired. A burning pain pierced her side as she fell on top of him.

"Jade!"

Sirens sounded in the distance, and their would-be robber flung the backdoor open and fled into the night.

Jade gasped for breath from the pain.

"Stay with me, baby!" Andrew had rolled so her back was on the floor. Shit. Had she been shot?

The blood sprinkled on Andrew's chest gave her pause.

"Open up! Police!"

"Get the door," she croaked. Andrew hurried to the foyer to let them in.

"They ran out the back. And they shot my girlfriend!"

The next thing Jade knew, a pair of paramedics were applying pressure, which equaled excruciating pain. When she could open her eyes through the agony, she caught glimpses of Andrew hovering in the background.

The team of first responders lifted her onto a gurney. Someone put an oxygen tube into her nose and threw a blanket over her. She managed to catch Andrew's eye before they wheeled her away. His mask had been stripped away. The fear etched on his face reminded her of the story about his high school sweetheart. Jade pressed her lips into a kiss and blew it at him. Right before she lost sight of her boyfriend, his shoulders dropped and his face relaxed.

She wasn't leaving him.

A shaky Andrew gave his statement of events to the police officers that responded to their call. Once the ambulance took Jade away, he wanted to get that part of the night out of the way so he could follow her to the hospital. The officer could have been the nicest person in the world, but Andrew couldn't have cared less.

It felt like this was happening to someone else. One minute, he was asleep, the next he was in a movie. Or maybe he was still dreaming. He pinched himself on the arm while the cop took notes. Damn, he was awake. What did dreaming about Jade and her late grandmother mean, anyway?

Another cop reentered the house through the back door. "Whoever they were, we lost them. They shed everything and ran." They carried a pile of black clothes that Andrew recognized as the ones the intruder had worn. "We'll send these off to forensics. Hopefully, there's a hair sample or something we can use to find your man."

Andrew just nodded as a numbness crept in around the edge of his brain.

After the police took their photos and taped up the window, the officer in charge broke the news to him. "You can't stay here while there's an ongoing investigation. Do you have somewhere else to go?"

He nodded. The hospital, for one. And then they could go back to Jade's hotel room before they went home.

"Thank you, officer." Andrew shook his head and offered his hand. The police officer shook it and they showed themselves out.

His bare feet pounded up the wooden steps two at a time. He had to get to Jade.

First, he stopped in the bathroom and heaved up what few contents lay in his stomach. Reminded that they didn't eat dinner, Andrew rinsed his mouth at the sink. That's when he caught sight of the blood spattered on his chest and side. Jade's blood.

Black circles teased at the edge of his vision, but he quickly sponged himself off with a washcloth. No way was he going into the emergency room with blood on him.

Calmer, now that the blood was gone, Andrew dressed quickly and gathered everything they had brought upstairs with them. Memaw's recipe book teased him from the nightstand under Jade's phone.

They wouldn't be able to come back for it until the cops took the crime scene tape down. Andrew wasn't willing to risk Jade losing her prize.

He found the keys to the rental in her purse downstairs. They'd need to hit a hardware store tomorrow and get some plywood to cover the window. In the meantime, he found a dusty tarp on the shelves, which he quickly taped over the hole to the outdoors. Then, finally, he shut off the lights and put everything into the car.

As he placed Jade's purse on the passenger seat, it lit up from within. He pulled out her cell phone. Mia was calling!

Oh fuck, he had to tell her friends what happened.

Andrew slid his thumb to answer the call.

"Hi, Mia."

"Andrew? Ah, I see you found Jade."

"Yeah, listen. She's been hurt."

The smugness drained from Mia's voice. Gasps punctuated his tale of their encounter with the mysterious stranger dressed in black.

"I'll call the girls. We'll be there by morning."

"Are you sure?"

"Positive. We're her only family."

I want to be her family. Andrew was startled at the thought.

"What do you need, Andrew?"

He'd come to New Orleans without even a stick of deodorant. "Can I give my brother your number so he can bring you some clothes for me? I wasn't thinking about that when I flew down here. I just drove straight to the airport."

Mia emitted a sound that sounded like a mix between a squeal and a squeak, before giving her assent. "Give me your number too, so I can reach you directly."

He rattled off his cell number. "Thanks, Mia. I'm on my way to the hospital now. I'll see you soon."

Pulling up the address the nice officer had written down for him, he plugged it into his GPS app and pulled away. Then he called Aiden on speaker.

"Dude, do you know what time it is?" His brother croaked.

"Listen, Jade's grandma died, and she had to deal with the house. We were sleeping in said house when someone broke in. She's been shot and I'm heading to the hospital now."

"Fuck!" The sleep fell from Aiden's voice, and Andrew could see him shooting up in bed, wide awake. "What do you need?"

"Her friends are on their way. I could use a change of clothes and some deodorant."

"You really ran to the airport with no preparation, didn't you?"

"Yeah, there are some carnations in my car that are probably wilted to hell."

Aiden chuckled. "Carnations? Dude, you shoulda bought roses."

Andrew sighed. "It made sense at the time."

"It's the thought that counts, right?"

"I hope so." He could always buy her more.

Chapter 18

ANDREW HAD FALLEN INTO a light sleep after sitting for hours in the hard plastic chairs of the emergency room waiting area. He'd tucked Jade's purse and shoes under his seat and leaned against a column. She'd been in surgery when he arrived, but the nurse had promised to come get him when she was admitted to a room. But that's not who woke him.

His mirror image hovered over him.

"Ai... dan?" he grunted.

"Andrew!" His unusually somber twin broke out into a smile so wide he could see both dimples.

"What are you doing here?"

"Mia invited us on the plane."

"Plane?"

"Yeah, apparently she knows someone with a private jet."

The girl in question came over with the squad in tow, as well as —

"Mom?"

Monica Monroe sniffed. "You didn't think Aiden was going to get all the fun, did you?"

"Who's running the club?"

Aiden waved him off. "It'll survive without the bosses for a night or two. Our people have things under control."

Andrew groaned and stretched his stiff muscles. "What a night. I could sleep for a week."

Aiden squeezed his shoulder. "Luckily, you're one of the bosses and you can take as long as you need."

"Jade?"

"She can take as much time as she needs, too." His mother patted his shoulder.

"No, I meant, does anyone know how she is?"

"She's still in recovery from surgery. We can wait here if you want to get food or something," said Rosie. "We told them she was our sister. I don't think they believed us," she added with a snicker.

His stomach chose that moment to growl.

"What time is it?"

"About six-thirty local time." Mia chimed in.

Andrew rubbed his eyes. He needed copious amounts of caffeine.

"Come on, Bro. I'm starving." Aiden threw his arm around Andrew as he stood up.

"Her shoes and purse are on the floor." He pointed as Aiden led him away.

"Got it!" Nadia gave him a thumbs up.

Mom flanked his other side, and they followed the signs to the cafeteria. His stomach might want food, but he had no idea what he wanted to eat. Nothing looked appetizing. Eventually, he settled on an egg and sausage bagel sandwich.

Thankfully, his mom and twin waited until they were seated around the table in more rigid plastic chairs before asking questions. He told them the story of their crazy night, minus the dream. The enormity of what Jade had done didn't fully hit him until he saw it in their eyes.

She'd taken a goddamn bullet for him.

"I'm going to throw that woman a damn parade." Monica covered her mouth and closed her eyes. "We could have lost you."

"I could have lost *her*, Mom." Andrew rubbed at the hollow feeling in his chest.

He almost had to laugh at the irony. He'd held himself back from her for so long to avoid her leaving him. And now he was totally invested.

"I still can't believe you jumped on a plane with nothing but the clothes on your back to get to her." Aiden shook his head and shoved another tater tot in his mouth. "That's not like you."

"Love makes you do crazy things." Monica eyed him knowingly over her cup of tea. "I'll expect you both at Sunday dinner next week."

A grin stretched across Andrew's face. "I should probably talk to her first."

"She doesn't know?"

He shrugged. "We haven't said the words yet."

"Get on that, Bro!"

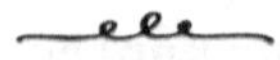

"There is a limit on the number of guests in the room, miss."

"*Fine.* You and Rosie take the first shift. Olivia and I will go grab something to eat. Text us if anything changes." That sounded like Nadia...

"You got it."

Where... where was she? The light was so bright her eyes hurt even when closed. Her chest ached and her throat felt like she'd swallowed razor blades. Groaning, Jade tried to shield her face with her hand, but it had something attached to it. The bite of a needle in her vein jolted her to full consciousness, and she squinted to see an IV in her arm.

"Jade! You're awake!" That was... Mia? Why would Mia be in New Orleans?

"Too... bright..." she croaked. Immediately, the lights dimmed, and she could open them. The pain was still there, but it was bearable.

Rosie and Mia ran straight to her bedside. "Where...?" *Damn,* it hurt to talk.

Shy, quiet, Rosie patted her hand. "You're in the hospital. In New Orleans. You got shot, Jade." The worry etched on Rosie's face made her look older than their twenty-five years.

Memories of the intruder flashed through her, and she groaned.

"They had to perform surgery to remove the bullet from your side. But it missed any vital organs."

That explained her fuzziness.

"Andrew?"

"He's taking his turn in the cafeteria." Mia said. "Olivia and Nadia will probably fight him to be back here first." Mia typed away at her phone.

All the stress of the situation hit Jade at once. Tears ran down her face and her breath came in short gasps. Mia grabbed a box of tissues. Rosie stroked a calming hand down her arm.

"Jade, honey, breathe. Should I ask the nurse to turn up your oxygen?"

She didn't know how to answer. All of her emotions were leaking from her eyes and she couldn't lift a damn finger.

Mia gently dried her cheeks while Rosie ran out of the room to look for her nurse.

"It's gonna be okay, sis. We got you."

Thank God for Andrew and her friends. Jade would have been completely alone in the world if it weren't for them.

Just then, an attendant came in with Rosie on her heels. "She was hyperventilating."

"Hi Jade. I'm Katie, your nurse for today. Are you having trouble breathing?"

Fuck *yes,* she was having trouble breathing. But all Jade could do was nod. Katie adjusted a lever on the tank at her bedside, and Jade's lungs eased a bit.

"Just rest for a while. Call me if you need anything else."

Andrew... she needed to see Andrew. But now that the oxygen was flowing freely, Jade couldn't keep her eyes open.

When Jade woke up the next time, she became aware of a warmth surrounding her hand. The light was dimmer, so it was easy to open her eyes and roll her head to the side. Sitting in a recliner pulled up next to her bed was Andrew.

He'd laid his head down at some point on the arm that held her hand. At some point, he'd changed clothes, and she wondered how. Clearing her throat, she squeezed his hand. His head jerked up and his gray eyes flew open.

"Hi," she croaked.

"Hi there." He grinned wide enough to put his dimples on display. "How are you feeling?"

"Like I got hit by a truck." She tried to swallow around her sandpaper tongue. "Is there any water?"

"Of course!" He jumped up, grabbed a plastic cup off the bedside tray, and put a straw in it for her.

The water tasted like heaven to her parched throat. She downed one glass quickly, and he refilled it from the pitcher on the table. The second went down slower, and when he held out a third, she shook her head.

Her primary concern was him. "Are you okay?"

"I'm fine." Andrew cupped her face with one hand and pressed his forehead to hers. "Thanks to you."

"Did the cops catch whoever broke in?"

He pressed his lips together, and she knew it was bad news. "No, baby, they didn't."

"Damn it."

"Forget them. I was so worried about you, Jade." He kissed her hard and fast, then gazed deep into her eyes. "I love you."

The flutters in her chest grew feathers and took flight. "I love you, too."

He pulled himself down to take her in his arms as best he could, and she wrapped her arms around him as well. "Don't you ever scare me like that again."

"Well, don't get a gun pulled on yourself, hmm?"

Andrew's deep chuckle soothed her nerves. "We're quite a pair, aren't we?"

"Mm-hmm." Then they were kissing, long and slow, like they'd been apart for months.

When they paused for air, Andrew pressed his forehead to hers. "I love you, Jade. I know this isn't romantic like you deserve, but I could have lost you without saying it at all. And I can't risk that happening again."

Jade's heart fluttered "I love you, too."

As she pulled him back down to kiss him again, a gasp from the doorway halted her. "She's awake!"

Jade broke the kiss, and Andrew stood up. "Come on in, Mia." He turned back to Jade and winked. "They only allow two visitors at a time, so I'll step out so your squad can take their turns."

Andrew looked over his shoulder as he passed Mia and Nadia on their way in.

"Hey, you." Mia skipped to her bedside.

"What are you guys doing here?"

"Your man answered your phone and told me what happened." Mia took Andrew's seat. "I called Howard and he let me borrow the plane."

Jade racked her brain, but she couldn't remember hearing that name before. "Who?"

"That's her step-dad." Nadia grinned. "We're all here. Mia even let Aiden and Monica hop a ride."

"Like I'm going to keep a woman from her son after a night like that." Mia gave Nadia an indignant look.

Jade chuckled. "Y'all didn't have to hop on a plane for me."

"Oh yeah? Try and stop us." Nadia folded her arms over her chest, her grin never waning.

"I'm glad you're here."

"Me, too. We'll send in Rosie and Olivia. I think Rosie is trying to interrogate the nursing staff again."

Shit, laughing hurt. But thinking of quiet, shy Rosie pestering the hospital workers was too funny.

"Yeah, let's give them a break." Mia rose from the recliner and patted her shoulder. "Let us know if you need anything."

"Maybe..." Ugh, she sounded like a frog. "You could take the hotel key and get my suitcase? And go use the bed. At least someone should sleep in it."

"It's in your purse?" Mia asked.

Jade just nodded, then took the water Nadia handed her.

"You got it, girl. We'll send the other two in."

Mia slipped the keycard into her pocket and her friends left the room.

Only a few minutes passed before Olivia and Rosie re-placed them.

"How's the hero feeling?"

Jade chuckled. "I've been better."

"I'm sure," Olivia leaned over the bed to give her a gentle hug.

"You been pestering my nurses?" Jade teased Rosie, who shrugged with no apology on her face.

"I told them we were family."

Jade raised an eyebrow.

"But I don't think they believed me." Rosie snickered and placed her ivory arm next to Jade's dark brown one.

"Mia mentioned something about adoption, so they let it slide." Olivia hid her giggle behind her hand.

Jade snorted and reached for her friends. "Thanks for coming."

"Wild horses couldn't keep us away." Olivia squeezed her hand.

"The boys and Marcia all say get well soon." Rosie smiled.

"Anyone say how long till I get out of here?"

"They'll probably want to make sure you can walk first. But the nurse said your post-surgery tests came back clear." Rosie shrugged. "I'm not used to adult care. My best guess is one more day."

"Speaking of walking," Jade shifted on the bed. "I need to pee."

Her stiff muscles protested as she swung her legs over the edge. Rosie and Olivia helped her drag the IV pole to the bathroom. After she did her business, she flipped her hospital gown up and checked out her bandage. Wearing a bra was going to be interesting.

Jade wandered the room a bit to stretch her legs. The wound on her side still stung, but it wasn't immobilizing.

Her friends only hovered a moment to be sure she was steady on her feet. "Can we bring you anything from the gift shop? They had some word searches."

"Or a book?" asked Rosie.

"Mia was going to get my suitcase from the hotel. I'd love some pajamas."

"Yeah, she bounced a few minutes ago." Olivia thumbed at the door.

Jade settled into the recliner and then noticed the television on the wall. "How do we turn this thing on?"

Rosie handed her a remote attached to the wall by a thick cord. "The buttons are all on there, and that's how you call for your nurse."

"Cool."

"You sure you don't want anything?"

"I should probably check my phone." Not that anyone would have called her.

Olivia handed it to her, anyway. "At least we can all message when we're not back here with you."

Jade leaned back against the chair. "You guys don't have to stay."

"What's the fun in working for myself if I can't take time off for important shit?" Olivia glared.

"What? You quit the station?" Last Jade checked, Olivia was still working her day job as a graphic designer at a local sports network, then going home to work on her freelance clients at night.

"Yup. It was way too much. I lost a lot of sleep and wasn't doing my best at any of my projects. So I handed in my two weeks and now I'm done!"

"That's awesome!" Jade got to her feet and hugged her friend. "I'm so happy for you."

"Thanks." Olivia pulled back so Rosie could hug her as well.

"Love your face. We'll see you later, okay? I'm sure Andrew wants to come back here."

"Yeah, probably."

Speaking of her boyfriend, he stuck his head in at the sound of his name.

"Jade? Is it okay if my mom and Aiden come in?"

"Sure!"

Olivia and Rosie waved as they left, and Andrew returned with his mom.

Monica rushed over and hugged her. "Oh my sweet girl, you had us worried!"

Jade patted her on the back. "I'm okay. Just sore."

"I bet you are." The older woman stood back up and wiped under her eyes. "I wanted to invite you over for dinner on Sunday. I've been waiting for Andrew to bring someone home for a long time."

"Ma!"

Jade chuckled at his embarrassment. "I'd love to."

"Wonderful!" Monica patted her son on his shoulder. "I'll send Aiden in."

Andrew stared down at her, then lifted her and sat back down in the recliner, settling her on his lap to her sheer delight.

"That's better." He grinned.

"You should go to my hotel room and get some sleep."

"Nah." He tightened his grip on her thighs. "I don't want to be apart from you."

"This chair can't be comfortable for sleeping."

Andrew just shrugged.

"Hey you two!" Aiden strode into the room. "Aren't you guys cozy?"

"Hi, Aiden." Jade replied. She could feel herself starting to droop. Apparently, she had already worn herself out.

Aiden seemed to sense her fatigue. "I just wanted to say thanks for pushing this idiot out of the way. And I'm sorry you got hurt." He placed a candy bar on the table. She recognized it as one they'd talked about at the office. "I got you a Milky Way for when you're feeling hungry. Hospital food is not known to be good. Later!" He backed out of the room like he was a teenager sneaking out.

Jade chuckled and leaned against the chair. Andrew laid a quick kiss on her neck. "You want to lay down?"

"No." She snuggled in. "I want you to hold me."

She groaned as her phone lit up.

"Ignore it baby."

"I can't. It's Memaw's lawyer." Jade swiped her thumb to answer. "Hi, Hilda."

"Hi, Jade. I'm afraid I have bad news."

Chapter 19

Jade cleared her throat. "What's up?"

"I just got a call from the police that your grandmother's house caught fire. They still listed the estate as the owner of record in their system, so they called me."

"What!" Jade covered her mouth as Andrew tightened his hold on her. "How?"

Hilda hesitated. "The investigation isn't complete yet."

Jade groaned. "Great. I wonder if this has anything to do with the break-in."

"Break-in?"

She proceeded to give Hilda a recap of their crazy night, ending with the fact she was speaking from the hospital.

"I can start the paperwork with the insurance company if you need me to."

"That would be great. If you could help me coordinate things from New Orleans, I'd appreciate it. I'd really like to get home." Jade laid her head down on Andrew's shoulder, who ran a gentle hand over her back.

"I can do that. Listen, you should know they suspect arson."

Her blood roared in her ears. "Ar—*arson*?"

"Yes. Apparently, the firefighters found evidence of an accelerant where the fire started in the kitchen. They were asking if Lou Ellen had any enemies. I had to tell them that the extended family was not pleased with the contents of the will. So I have to provide a list of relatives. That doesn't mean it was any of them, but they may be suspects."

That made sense. Although she had thought they would only contest the will, not burn her inheritance. But then again, these *were* her relatives. It wasn't that much of a stretch to decide to take it from the abomination in any way possible. And burning it to the ground was cheaper than hiring an attorney.

This was all too much. Finding out about Memaw's death, and then inheriting everything, had been over-whelming enough, without Andrew showing up to make amends. Thank goodness he had, and she hadn't been alone going through the house. But now the stress caught up to her; Jade's pulse beat a steady tempo in her head.

"Anyway, I will keep you posted."

"Sounds great. Thank you so much, Hilda." They hung up, and Jade cradled her head in her palms. "You hear all that?"

Andrew kept rubbing her back, which normally would make Jade want to purr like a cat. "The house is gone?"

She nodded. "It caught fire. Burned down and they suspect arson."

"Did you say arson?" Nadia poked her head inside the hospital room.

"Yeah. The house burned down last night. Firefighters found an accelerant." Jade blinked back tears. They were just things. But they were all she had left of her Memaw.

Olivia let out a whistle from the hallway.

"What the *fuck*?" cried Rosie.

All heads snapped to watch their favorite nurse behind her friends. Nadia was the first to recover. "Hang on a second. Did you just *curse*?" Rosie had been raised by her grandparents and she *never* swore. *Ever.*

Shy, sweet, innocent Rosie just shrugged. Then her face turned bright red. "Don't make such a big deal out of it, okay?"

Exhausted as she was, Jade clapped her hands. "Sugar, I'm so *proud* of you!"

Rosie hid behind her hands. "Shut up."

Olivia whipped out her cell. "I have to text Matt."

"No!" Rosie reached for Olivia's phone, but couldn't get to it. "You can't tell him!"

"I have to tell him he's doing a good job!"

"You mean you're going to tell him he's a bad influence?"

Olivia shrugged, still holding her phone out of reach. "To-may-to, to-mah-to."

Jade seized her sides as laughter erupted from her belly, her eyes watering. Leave it to her friends to distract her from all her problems. Jade could see now she'd never truly been alone.

Nadia wheeled Jade's suitcase into the room. "Mia said to drop this off. She's in the little girls room."

Clothes! Jade lifted herself to her feet with Andrew's assistance. "Thanks, Nad. Shut the door so I can put some pants on, okay?"

"Sure. We'll be out in the waiting room razzing Rosie. Text us if you need us."

Rosie glared at Nadia, red-faced. "Hey!"

Nadia just laughed as the door closed.

Andrew lifted the suitcase onto the bed so Jade could open it.

"I kinda like this easy-access thing." He teased the edges of her gown where it gapped in front of her ass.

Jade swatted his hands away from her behind as she hunted for her pajama pants. She pulled the super soft fabric over her hips and sighed.

"Nice. I love those."

"Thanks." They were her favorite pair of lounge pants, pink with old-school comic book sayings like "POW" and "BAM" printed all over.

"Why don't you lay down and rest, love?" Andrew zipped her suitcase and set it back on the floor.

A knock came at the door. "What now?"

"Hi Jade, I'm here to do a vitals check on you." Jade's nurse aide entered the room with the blood pressure cuff. She sat on the bed and dutifully let him take her temperature and blood pressure.

When the thermometer left her mouth, she asked the question at the forefront of her mind. "Any idea when it's safe for me to get out of here?"

The man chuckled and programmed her readings into the computer. "I'll talk to your nurse. She can ask the doctor."

"Okay, thanks."

⁓ℓℓ⁓

Andrew roused from an uncomfortable night atop the wretched recliner around seven in the morning when the nurses came in for shift change. He stretched and sighed, looking over at Jade, who slept on. She had sent her friends to the hotel to get some sleep, but Andrew refused to leave her. From what Aiden had told him about their trip, he'd be able to sleep just fine on the plane.

They'd taken her off the oxygen last night and she seemed much better.

When the staff left, he busied himself with freshening up in the bathroom, then changed into another set of clothes in the bag from his brother. Jade woke up when he reentered, so he bussed a quick kiss on her cheek.

"Good morning, beautiful."

"Mm, good morning."

"How are you feeling?"

She sat up and swung her legs over the bed. "Better. Need to pee."

"It's all yours." He gestured at the open bathroom door. "I'm gonna head down to the cafeteria for some breakfast. You want anything?"

"They'll bring me breakfast. Don't worry about it." She dragged the IV pole to the door, then shut it around the tubing.

"I'll be right back."

By the time Andrew returned with his bagel sandwich and crappy hospital coffee, Jade's tray had arrived. They sat and ate together in contented silence.

"How did you sleep?"

Andrew shrugged. "I slept fine."

"That can't be comfortable." Jade snorted in disbelief.

"I wouldn't have slept at all if I wasn't next to you." He reached over and tucked a stray braid behind her ear. She smiled and pressed her cheek into his touch.

After breakfast, they found a channel showing the old X-Men cartoon and sat there picking it apart together.

"Comics are so much better," Jade murmured as a knock came on the door. She muted the television as a young Asian guy in a white coat entered the room.

"Good morning, Miss Aguillard. How are you feeling? I'm Dr. Park, I'm part of the care team here."

"I'm feeling pretty good."

"Great! Can I take a peek under your bandage? Then we can discuss getting you out of here."

"Music to my ears, sugar." Jade laid down on her good side and flipped the hospital gown up so Dr. Park could access her surgical site.

"Hmm... yes, it looks like you're healing fine. Do you have someone to help you change the bandage daily?"

Andrew raised his hand. "I volunteer as tribute."

Jade cocked an eyebrow at him. "You know three of my friends live in the same building as me, right? And one of them is a nurse?"

"You're not getting rid of me that easily, baby. I can stay with you, or you can stay with me. I don't care which."

Dr. Park smirked. "I'll put in the order for discharge. Whoever you want to help with the bandage will need to be here so we can teach them how to care for the surgery site."

"Will I need to find a doctor to get the stitches out back home?"

"No, we used dissolving stitches, so you won't need them taken out." Dr. Park replaced the bandage and laid Jade's gown back in place. "Have a great day, Miss Aguillard."

They zoned out in front of the television for a few hours until the nurse came in with Jade's walking papers.

Shannon showed Andrew how to change Jade's bandages and advised him to change it daily. "It has to be kept dry," she continued. "So sponge baths only for the first week."

Jade made a face and Andrew kept his chuckle to himself. He could make those fun for her.

She turned to Jade. "If it swells, you can apply ice. And you need to keep it elevated."

He could order some more pillows on Prime.

She sent them home with a bag of bandages and gauze. Andrew breathed a sigh of relief as they headed for the elevators at last. But Jade seemed lost in thought.

"Happy to be going home?"

"Of course!" She gave him an absent-minded kiss on the cheek as they got into the elevator.

They ran into their entourage in full force down in the lobby. "Ready to blow this popsicle stand?" Mia asked her. His girl hesitated.

"Can... Can we go by the house first? I need to see it."

Andrew wasn't sure this was a good idea. "Are you sure that's what you want?"

She nodded with vigor. "I need to know if there's anything left."

His mind strayed to the gray binder zipped safely in his suitcase. Which was now buried under the other luggage in the rental.

"If you're sure." Mia squeezed Jade's shoulder. "I'll call the pilot when we're on the way."

"Pilot?"

Mia turned around with a giggle. "Yeah. Turns out my new step-dad is pretty awesome."

They left the hospital in two vehicles. Andrew sat with his arm around Jade in the backseat of the SUV. Mia drove with Nadia next to her, while his mom followed in another rental with Aiden, Rosie, and Olivia. *Here goes nothing.*

Chapter 20

He wasn't sure what to expect when they arrived at Jade's ancestral home. But nothing could have prepared Andrew for the blackened, hollowed-out shell that greeted them.

The front of the house was the least damaged, but the door was wide open, letting them see the burnt-out hallway behind strips of yellow caution tape. Where a wall between the stairs and the kitchen once stood was now a ragged hole.

"We would have been in there," Jade sobbed, pulling his attention away from what could have been their tomb. She trembled with her realization, her eyes fixed on her childhood home. He swept in front of her, putting himself between her and the building; this was a bad idea. Wrapping her up in a tight embrace, he rubbed her back and tried to soothe her.

He pressed a kiss to her temple as her friends gathered to comfort her, placing them in the center of a squad group hug. No one said a word or cracked a joke about their PDA.

"What do you want to do, Jade?" Mia asked gently.

"There's nothing left. Let's just go home."

Andrew tightened his arms around her. "That's not true, baby. I got your recipes." Her head snapped up, red-rimmed eyes blinking. "They're in my suitcase in the car. I put the binder in the rental when I left for the hospital."

"Oh my God!" She buried her face in his chest again and her tears spread across his shirt. "You're amazing. Th-thank you."

He carefully maneuvered her so her back faced the house, murmuring in her ear as everyone piled into the cars. "Let's go pack you a bag. You can stay at my place and we'll go through the book and make up whatever you want, okay?"

Jade nodded against his chest and he had her buckled in no time, as Mia spoke with the pilot. When her call was done, she hopped into the driver's seat and headed for the airport.

Instead of going to the regular airport, Mia drove to a small private airfield. She handed the keys to the rentals to two employees while others gathered their bags. The entire group filed out to a plane sitting on the tarmac with *McCleary Industries* painted on it in gold.

Silence reigned supreme on the flight back. Most of the passengers slept. About halfway there, Andrew leaned over and whispered to Jade, asking if she needed to talk. Jade just shook her head and continued staring out the window at the clouds rolling by. A squeeze of his hand reassured him.

He wished he could carry some of this stress for her. But he couldn't take anything off her shoulders unless she let him.

And after their near-death experience, he didn't want to leave her side.

When they were coming in for a landing, Andrew reached for his love. "Will you come home with me, Jade?" Her deep brown eyes looked at him with one eyebrow raised. "Please?"

She licked her lips and seemed to understand what he was asking. "Yeah, sugar. I'd love to."

He grinned and wrapped an arm around her shoulders. "You'll be lucky if I don't move you in. I don't want to let you out of my sight."

Jade snuggled in tight and laid her head on his shoulder. "The feeling is mutual."

Warmth settled into his chest as the pilot made the approach.

After picking his Explorer up from the parking garage, he drove to her place so she could fill her suitcase with about a week's worth of clothes. When she dumped her dirty clothes into the hamper, he lifted the basket.

"What are you doing?"

"You don't want to do laundry at my place?"

"Won't your neighbors be mad?"

Andrew grinned. "Baby, I have in-unit laundry. No one cares."

"Ooh you fancy. Aight."

Relief flooded him as he glimpsed some of her normal sass peeking out.

He carried the hamper, and she thumped her luggage down the stairs. Then he turned the radio on for the drive to his place.

Andrew insisted on carrying her dirty laundry up in his elevator along with his suitcase, refusing Jade's offer of help. She realized in the time they dated, they'd always ended up at her place. He lived in a pricey-looking high rise not too far from the club. Everything was clean and modern.

He opened the door to his apartment, and Jade stood in the foyer and stared. His place had two-story ceilings and a wide open-concept kitchen and living room. Black leather couches paired with metal and glass furniture screamed masculinity.

Damn, this place needed a woman's touch.

She followed him back to the bedroom after kicking off her shoes, noting he dropped her hamper in front of a door next to the kitchen. *Must be the laundry room.*

His bedroom was a little more homey. A couple of framed photos of his family stood on the black wood dresser. A cozy blue comforter lay on the neatly made bed.

Andrew pulled some towels out of his own laundry basket and showed her the bathroom. A large walk-in shower in pristine white tile took up the entire back wall, then there was the toilet and a double vanity sink along the side wall.

"What do you feel like doing?" He asked her.

"I want to shower and sleep for a week, but I can't. I have to take sponge baths." Jade grimaced.

"Can I help you? I could wash your back."

She nodded and started warming up the water in the sink. Jade lined her body wash and hair care products along the back of the white vanity.

Taking her shirt off turned out to be a challenge. With Andrew's help, she pulled her arms inside the t-shirt and he pulled it off. "Looks like I'll have to go back and get my work clothes."

He grinned and waggled his eyebrows. "Or you could wear my shirts."

"Caveman," Jade scoffed.

She pulled her braids up out of the way, and let Andrew's gentle touch wash the dirt away, careful not to get her bandage wet. He even used one of those fluffy towels to pat her dry.

His lips ghosted over her legs, chasing the towel as he dried her off. Then a languid Jade leaned against the wall as Andrew dropped the towel to the floor and pressed light, teasing kisses up her thighs.

Still, she had to sass him. "I just got clean," she whined.

"And now I'm going to dirty you up again." His enormous hands gripped her hips. "Missed you."

"Need you." It had been too long since they'd been intimate and Jade hungered.

Andrew made eye contact from where he crouched, holding her gaze while he deliberately, gently, flicked the very tip of his tongue over her dick/clit, and her hips bucked towards his face. Grinning wickedly, Andrew placed one large hand above her pelvis and continued his oral assault on her nub.

Her back arched as a wildfire built in her blood, spreading out from her center to her fingertips and curling toes. Then her whole body tensed and she cried out her release as Andrew licked up the drips that leaked from her.

When she'd caught her breath, she realized he was still fully clothed while she was naked.

"Someone's overdressed for this party," she teased.

Andrew rose, his dimples popping in both cheeks. "I didn't want you to miss the show." He crossed his arms and lifted his shirt above his head, and Jade licked her lips at his flexed biceps and the forearms highlighted by his Celtic armband. One of these days, she was going to map those freckles all over his chest.

Then he shoved his sweatpants down those thick thighs, and she realized he was commando tonight.

Andrew stroked his length as he looked longingly up and down her body. "Where do you want me?"

Now it was her turn to tease. "Let me return the favor," she said as she sank to her knees on the towel. She gripped the base of his shaft and slowly circled her tongue around the head, but watched his face. His eyes rolled back in bliss as she worked him up, and when he whimpered, she took pity on him and swallowed his cock. Then she was working him over, coating him in her saliva on the way down, and hollowing out her cheeks and sucking as she pulled away. His thighs were just starting to quiver under her hands when he cried, "Wait!"

"What?" Was he serious?

Andrew hauled her up and kissed her, pouring his passion into her mouth. When he let her up for air, she tried to blink away her daze. Then his fingers drifted down her spine and over her puckered hole, and it twitched in anticipation.

"I need you. Please?"

She leaned into his hard, muscular chest and sucked at the pulse point on his neck. "Take me to bed, Andrew."

He whisked her off into his bedroom, laid her down, and climbed on top. She pulled him down for a kiss, needing to feel his weight on her, grinding together. The drawer in his nightstand slid open and shut with a soft click, then Andrew's fingers spread cold liquid over her rosette. She clenched initially, then relaxed as he continued to caress her. Slowly he teased her, opening her up gently first with one finger, then with two.

When he started scissoring his digits and spreading her wide, she broke the kiss. "Andrew," she pleaded, but he knew what she needed. He sat up on his knees and reached for the condom he'd laid on the bed, but she stilled his hand.

"We don't need it."

He looked down in shock. "Are you — are you sure?"

Biting her lip, Jade nodded. "There's no one else."

Wide-eyed, he ran a palm over his hair. "I've never had sex without one."

"Then we're safe, silly."

Andrew's hand shook as he lubed his dick, while his eyes focused on her. Jade pulled her knees back as far as they could go. He gripped his shaft at the base and placed it against her hole, then hesitated. "You're sure?"

"Please, take me bare."

"I love you." He pushed past the outer ring of muscles and then into her ass. "Jade!"

"Don't stop!"

They shivered in unison at the sensation of skin on skin. Electricity tickled her all over as he started to move. Their gazes locked together, and they moved as one, and she lost all track of time.

After she was nothing but a puddle of nerve endings, Andrew shuddered as his control broke. Picking up speed, he hit her P-spot repeatedly. Her nails dug into his shoulders as she clenched on his cock. Bliss overcame her as the second orgasm of the night washed over her with a shout. Then hot liquid spurted into her channel as Andrew moaned her name on repeat.

He caught his breath, slid out and snuggled up, his stubble tickling her neck. "That was... wow."

She chuckled. "Wow indeed."

Andrew shook his head and chuckled. "Aiden almost didn't recognize my reckless ass at the hospital."

"What?" Jade turned to him, her brows drawn together in confusion. "You? Reckless? Never!"

He pulled out of her with a sly smile, lifting one corner of his mouth. "Only for you."

She crossed her arms and raised an eyebrow, waiting for an explanation.

So Andrew started counting off on his fingers. "First, I approached you at my club, which I never do. Second, I broke my personal rule about dating employees. And third, I jumped on a plane to NOLA with nothing but the clothes on my back."

Jade grinned as he helped her off the bed, and they cleaned up in the bathroom. She slipped on her underwear and her Wonder Woman sleep shirt, sliding her legs under the covers while he opened his suitcase.

"At least I salvaged this."

Jade gasped, covering her mouth with her palms, as he pulled out a gray, tattered binder full of recipes made with love. He laid it gently in her lap, and she hovered her hands over it. He'd mentioned it back at the house, but part of her hadn't fully believed Memaw's recipe book had escaped her home's fate.

"Go ahead, baby, it's yours." He sat on the edge of the bed.

Jade hugged it gingerly to her chest as she teared up. "Thank you," she choked out, then flung herself into his open arms and drenched his shoulder.

Eventually, she wiped her eyes, but she stayed in his embrace. "She protected us."

Andrew stilled his hands. "What do you mean?"

Jade took a deep breath. "This is going to sound weird. But keep in mind, I know my Memaw." He nodded and waited for her to continue. "I had a dream about her and you in the living room. She looked so... healthy. Like she'd never been sick. You two were laughing, and I walked in late. Then she said, 'It's time to go. You're not supposed to be here.' Something like that. And she was telling me to wake up. 'Wake up, child!' Like I was late for school or something. Then I heard her *outside of* the dream. I woke up and heard the window break." She watched his eyes. Would he think she was crazy?

Andrew only tightened his hold on her. "I was there. It's... fuzzy, but I was in the dream with you."

"I don't think it was a dream at all." Jade bit her lip.

"You think that's where she is?" His eyes turned molten, and he pressed his forehead to hers. "That was really her." Jade nodded. "What else did she say?"

She snorted. "That it was about time I brought someone home." Her features softened into a dreamy look. "I think she likes you. I just wish I knew what y'all were talking about when I came in."

Her man grew thoughtful, and she could almost see the wheels turning.

"I don't remember exactly what we said. But I have the general gist."

He pulled his arms back from Jade and gripped her hands even as they held Memaw's recipes tight. "Jade?"

"Yeah?"

"I have... one more reckless thing I want to do."

She looked at him incredulously. "What can be more reckless than hopping on a plane with nothing packed?"

He waited for a heartbeat, then slid off the bed and lowered himself to one knee in front of her, never taking his gaze from hers.

"You are the strongest, most amazing woman I've ever met. I love you with all my heart, and I would go through everything all over again just to be right here with you. This crazy trip has driven home to me how quickly everything can be taken from us, and I don't want to wait when I know what I want. Jade Aguillard, will you marry me?"

Jade's heart stopped and her mouth gaped as she gazed into melted steel eyes, so full of love and promises. He wanted to *marry* her?

He must have mistaken her silence for reluctance. A blush rose to color his tawny cheeks. "I was planning to wait until I got a ring, but I just — I just can't wait any longer and I had to ask. If that's not what you want, I'm not going anywhere, I still love—"

She cut him off with a kiss, gripping his face in both hands. When she released him, she pressed their foreheads together and answered him. "My answer is yes!" Her heart was bursting with joy.

"Really?"

Jade nodded, tears of joy streaming down her face. Somehow, she knew Memaw was watching them and smiling.

Andrew turned off the light and climbed into the other side of the bed. He gathered her in his arms and spoke in her ear. "Wanna shop for a ring tomorrow?"

"I kinda promised Nadia I'd go out with her tomorrow." Jade bit her lip. "After?"

"That works." He flipped the blanket up over them. "Let's get you some rest, like the doctor ordered."

She suspected they wouldn't be getting as much sleep as they were supposed to.

Epilogue

Finally, life had returned to normal. Well, normal outside of driving Jade to and from work. Andrew reached over the console and picked up his fiancée's hand to kiss the knuckle above the dainty diamond ring she'd selected from the antique shop.

"Charmer. I'm still not breaking my lease."

"It'd save on gas money."

"Unless I buy a car."

Her grandmother's old clunker hadn't passed inspection, and it would have cost more than it was worth to get the repairs done. So Jade sold it off, but still hadn't gone car shopping. She was waiting for the insurance check to come through on the house. Which was waiting for the arson investigation.

And who knew how long *that* would take?

She'd won the argument about Andrew opening her car doors for her. But she had agreed to wait for him in the event of a special occasion. He thought every day with her was a special occasion, but she had outmaneuvered him.

Taking her hand, they walked into the office together, only to be accosted by Aiden at the top of the stairs.

"Thank God you're here! Ember's coming up and she'll need the moral support."

"Moral support? For what?" Jade took the words right out of Andrew's mouth.

Aiden bounced on the balls of his feet. "We got him on camera!"

"For real?" Andrew asked.

"She hasn't identified him yet, but based on how he harassed someone at the bus stop, I'm willing to bet it's him."

Ember came in shortly after them, a police officer behind her.

"This is Detective Wells. He's been working on my case."

"I heard you may have security footage of this guy?"

"Yes, sir. That's why I asked Ember to come in early."

Ember gnawed on her lip as everyone gathered in Aiden's office. Andrew and Jade flanked her as Aiden called up the footage. "Someone flagged down our guards about one-thirty when this started, so that's how I knew where to look." His twin flipped his laptop around so they could see without crowding behind his desk. "I'm starting it at the time our patron entered the bus shelter."

A drag queen Andrew recognized from a show he attended during Pride came on screen dressed to the nines, waving to her friends out of view. When a white male in a black hooded sweatshirt snuck up behind her, Ember gasped.

"That's him!" She shielded her eyes. "Stop it, Aiden, *please!*"

Jade threw an arm over Ember's shoulders as Aiden paused the video and flipped his laptop back to face him. She murmured soothing words to their coworker and friend, encouraging her to breathe deeply.

"Can I get a copy of that from you, sir?" asked the detective. He gave Aiden his business card.

"Is she okay?" Ember inquired in a panic.

Aiden nodded as he typed. "She's fine. She threatens him with mace and Nolan comes running up, but he ran off."

"We'll run it through facial recognition software, and it will be enough to get a warrant. You'll still need to come in to identify him in a line-up." He looked at Ember with sympathy.

Ember shivered, but agreed.

"One of us can go with you." Jade told her, looking up at Andrew. He nodded and gripped his friend's shoulder.

"Thank you, Detective." Andrew and Aiden shook Detective Wells's hand, letting Jade offer Ember comfort.

He had never seen Ember so shaken. "Why don't you head home for a bit and relax before your shift?"

"That sounds like a good idea." Ember said, rising. "I'll see you guys later."

Andrew and Jade both took deep breaths, then embraced. He'd feel much better once this asshole was off the streets and far away from his girl.

"Can y'all hug it out in your own office?" Aiden pretended to gag. "I don't need to see this."

"Like you and Jeff aren't just as bad," Andrew teased. "Come on, Jade. I want some coffee."

"I might require something stronger." She shook her head as she preceded him out of his brother's space.

In the break room, Andrew pulled her into his arms and held on tight. It was awful enough that the attack happened to his friend. He didn't know what he'd do if that had been Jade.

"You okay?" Concern marred her face.

"Yeah, I just need to hold you for a minute."

"Okay." She laid her head on his shoulder. "I'm not complaining, but we do have to work."

"I know." He sighed. "I keep thinking, what if it had been you?"

Jade snorted. "I would have kicked his ass."

"But you shouldn't have to."

"No one should have to. No one should do what he's been doing. But I could have handled it. I've got more than a few inches on the guy."

He shuddered at the thought. "Even still. I don't think my heart could take it." He'd failed River by landing in detention and not walking them home the night of the attack. They'd never spoken to him again. It had terrified him into believing that if someone he cared about got hurt, then they would leave him. What he felt for River had been a drop in the ocean compared to what he felt for Jade. He couldn't lose her.

But then again, Ember was still around, despite being attacked on his property. He'd let her down, too. "You... You wouldn't leave me?"

"Of course not!" Jade's eyes bulged. "Why on Earth would I?"

"I think because River left when they were ambushed and I wasn't there to defend them, that I automatically need to protect anyone I care about, so they don't take off." God, saying out loud, it sounded so stupid.

"Andrew." He pulled back, and she cupped his chin. "River was a kid. They were hurting and lashed out, but what happened to them was *not your fault*. If I got hurt, it wouldn't be your fault, either. *Ember* getting attacked was not your fault. It's the fault of those football players and the guy lurking around the club. There will always be people who want to hurt us. But I don't need you to be my protector; I want you to be my partner.

"I'm not going anywhere, sugar." She assured him, wiping tears off his cheek. "I promise. I won't run off like that again." He turned his head and kissed her palm. "Maybe you should go home, too. This has you so upset."

"I'll be fine. Just come into my office for a minute?" At her look, he shook his head. "We're not doing anything frisky. I want to hold you on my lap for a bit and since I'm the boss, I can." Andrew wiped the tears off his face and pulled her into his office, where he did just that.

⁓

Months later, back in New Orleans, Jade sat in the Juvenile Justice Intervention Center with Andrew by her side. She'd left her engagement ring in the hotel safe, since the center had strict rules regarding what they allowed in the door. She had even steamed her new suit that morning in the room when she got up at five and couldn't get back to sleep.

A gray-haired battleship of a social worker met them at the gate. Elma was a rotund white woman who looked fifty but acted sixty, her unforgiving profession having taken its toll. She was the one that had arranged this meeting at Jade's request. Unusual, but Jade needed closure on what happened to Memaw's house and her harrowing experience.

An alarm sounded as the door at the other end of the room unlocked, and a correctional officer led a swaggering teen in an orange jumpsuit to the table in the center. Her cornrows framed a round, dark brown face with dull eyes. If it hadn't been for the name in the police report, Jade would have never recognized little Maya.

She'd only been eight years old when Jade came out of the closet. Her cousin's daughter used to beg her to play dolls and dress up with her. It had fulfilled Jade's own desires but let her pass it off to her dad as just entertaining the younger cousin. How had that bright-eyed girl with her braids and hair bows grown into a sullen teen arsonist?

The officer linked Maya's handcuffs to a ring in the middle of the table. Elma had warned Jade so she wouldn't be surprised. Apparently, she wasn't known for her good behavior.

"Miss Aguillard," Elma started. "you have a visitor."

Maya eyed them up but said nothing.

"I'm your cousin Jade." She let that sit for a second. "Leroy's youngest. We used to play dolls when you were a kid."

At that, Maya glared at her with suspicion. "I don't have a cousin Jade."

Jade nodded. "Right. Because I got kicked out of the family when you were eight." At Maya's confusion, she continued. "You were so young, you might not even remember. I went to live with Memaw when I was sixteen."

She looked away, still glowering.

"I miss her, too." Jade swallowed. "So why did the police call me and say you burned her house down?"

"Because I did."

"Why, Maya? Why would you destroy everything?"

"Because it should have been *ours*!" The chain linking her cuffs snapped taut as Maya jerked in her seat. "I *hate* you!"

Jade sat there and let her words wash over her. "I was going to have the lawyer call everyone and tell them to take whatever they wished from the house. You could have had anything you wanted to remind you of Memaw. But the fire destroyed it. It ruined everything before I opened it up." Maya's lip quivered, but she still wouldn't look at Jade.

Her cousin's breaths came short and fast. At seventeen, the state could try her as an adult, especially with the severity of the charges she faced.

"I... I ruined everything."

Elma waved to the security officer, who escorted Maya out. Jade gripped Andrew's hand tightly, wishing she could comfort the child she used to know.

When Maya was gone, Elma turned to her. "Are you sure you want to go through with it?"

Jade looked at Andrew, who nodded.

"Yes." She was more determined than ever to convince the district attorney to drop the attempted manslaughter charges.

"She will still almost certainly do time for the arson, as well as breaking and entering."

"But it won't be a life sentence." Jade wanted her little cousin to learn a lesson, not throw her future away. Her next victim might not be so lenient, but Jade couldn't bear to have this on her conscience.

Ultimately, the blame lay with Maya's parents. They had taught her to hate people who were different.

Back outside in the December sun, Andrew pulled Jade into his arms. "I'm proud of you. You didn't have to face her."

"She's just a kid."

"I realize that." He released her, and they walked hand in hand to the rental car.

"If she'd known we were in the house, I wouldn't drop the charges. But she had no idea. That was obvious when you surprised her in the kitchen."

Andrew opened the passenger door to their SUV, and she was too emotionally drained to argue. "Would it have changed anything?"

Jade shrugged. "We'll never know. I just hope she turns out okay."

Lights flashed to the DJ's beat, lighting up the Neon Unicorn dance floor in a rainbow of colors. The disco ball above spun squares of light over the writhing bodies. Andrew had Jade in his arms for the first annual New Year's Eve Bash.

It had been Aiden's idea to reward the staff, but when Andrew pointed out how few of them there were, he'd suggested selling tickets to the public. The DJs had volunteered to spin the music, coming up with their own scheduled slots so everyone could party. Employees of the actual club weren't on duty, instead the ticket money had gone to cover the cost of food, drinks, and hiring temporary security and bartenders. Nadia's older brothers were all there, hired through the eldest's company, Hunt Security. All the squad had told him was that the three rather intimidating men were various flavors of military, and that if he hurt Jade, no one would find his body.

Jade bumped and ground her ass into his hard cock. That liquid mercury dress slid under his hands, reminding him of the night they'd met. He nuzzled into the space behind her ear, the gentle coils of her hair tickling his cheek. Gone were her braids as Jade embraced the natural look. She'd said it had to do with giving up on bottom surgery; he would have supported her either way. But she was beautiful in her pure state, and he told her so regularly.

"I want to do something reckless," he spoke into her ear. She shuddered in his arms and he saw her nipples pebble beneath the fabric of her dress. Yes, no bra. He ran a palm over her breast, rubbing right over her peak. She gasped and spun around.

"Wanna fuck me in your office again?" Yeah, that had happened. More than once. But Andrew wanted to live out a different fantasy. He hoped she was on board.

"Can't wait that long," he spoke into her ear over the music. "Supply closet?"

Jade pulled back and stared incredulously at him. He raised an eyebrow. If she wasn't interested, he'd let it go.

Instead, she grabbed his hand and pulled him towards the hallway, past the people dancing. When they got to the shadowy passage, he pushed her into the wall and kissed her hard, her mouth welcoming his tongue as they started a new dance.

She set him on fire with her touch as her hands roamed. By the time they made it inside the closet, his shirt hung loose from his shoulders, her long dark fingers tracing the muscles he still took time to work on. He hiked up her dress and leaned over to suck her nipples into his mouth one by one, stopping her from pulling his trousers down. The beat of the music penetrated even in this little corner, but her moans were what he really wanted to hear.

He pulled the packet of lube and travel-size wet wipes out of his pants, then let them drop to the floor. Jade pulled her panties down and turned, presenting her ass to him as she leaned against the door. Andrew got his fingers slick and traced her rim, then teased her with one finger till she was pressing back for more.

"Get in there, damn it!"

Chuckling, he plunged two digits in, then three as she moaned, pegging her prostate like he knew she liked.

"I need your cock, sugar. Give it to me!"

How he loved it when she talked dirty. He'd really wound her up on the dance floor. Lubing his dick with the rest of the packet, Andrew pressed inside. God, she was so tight. He would never get enough of this. Reaching around to muff her in the front with one hand and tweak her nipples with the other, their carnal moans almost drowned out the shouts from the club.

"Ten... Nine..."

Andrew's thrusts sped up, his spine tingling, and Jade's cries grew frantic.

"Three... Two... One!"

Those fireworks he always got with her exploded behind his eyes as Jade shook with her own orgasm. They leaned against the closed door to catch their breath.

"Happy New Year, baby." He laid a gentle kiss on her smile.

"Happy New Year indeed."

Epilogue 2

ONE YEAR LATER

The cacophony of barks, yips, and howls assaulted Jade's ears as she followed Andrew back into the shelter.

"Let's just see if anyone jumps out at us."

A pit bull leaped up against the bars of its kennel, barking in deep tones, and startled her. "How... literally do you mean that?"

He chuckled and grabbed her hand. "Not like that. Let's find one that speaks to us."

"If we find a talking dog, I'm calling the mental ward."

His bright white grin reminded her why she'd agreed to this in the first place. After an exhausting house hunt, a four-bedroom house in his parents' neighborhood had come on the market, and they'd just closed two months ago and moved in. *This house is perfect for a dog,* he'd said when they toured it. *"We can set up a run or add a fence."* But ever since they moved in together last June, Andrew had talked about how much he wanted a dog. Now that he was working more normal hours at the club, and they had a home more suited for it, Jade had agreed that they could look into getting a dog.

Andrew had a dog growing up, but she never had. "Remember, I'm not picking up poop. That's your job."

"I got it, baby. Oh! This one looks like Bandit." He crouched down in front of a black lab, who jumped at him and looked like she wanted to lick his face.

Jade kept wandering down the aisle. So many dogs of all shapes and sizes fought for anyone's attention. Each one had a sign on their kennel with their name, approximate age, and any health issues.

One quiet kennel in the corner caught her attention. A medium-sized brown dog with ears halfway between pointy and floppy, lay curled up in the corner on her dog bed. Her eyes watched Jade carefully as she lifted the card to read her name, and Jade's heart skipped a beat.

Andrew found her then, with a volunteer right behind him. "Hey baby, who'd you find?"

"Her name is Lou Ellen." When Andrew didn't recognize it, she elaborated. "Memaw's name." She blinked back the tears pricking her eyelids. Andrew laid a hand on her shoulder.

"She's one of our seniors.," the volunteer accompanying them said. "Been here a while. No one ever tries to see her."

Andrew glanced at the card as well. "She's ten years old. What happened?"

The young woman shrugged. "Apparently, her owner died, and the family didn't want her. So they brought her here." Lou Ellen lifted her head, and Jade spied a pink pillow between her paws. "All she had was her collar and that pillow."

"Can we see her?" The words flew from Jade's mouth before she realized it. The volunteer hurried to unlock the kennel door.

"She won't come out, but you can go in. Just let her come to you. She hasn't let anyone pet her at all yet."

Lou Ellen whined as the door opened. Jade and Andrew slid down and sat against the wall opposite where the dog lay, watching them.

"Hi, sweetheart." Jade and Andrew kept their voices soft. They told her about the club, and the new house, and their friends. Jade sympathized with the dog; after all, most of her family had thrown her away, too.

Jade lost track of time as they talked about everything and nothing with this sweet animal. She was a good listener, and apparently liked their voices, because she lifted her head off her pillow to sniff Jade's hand. She didn't get close enough to pet, but Andrew spied something on the pillow.

"Look, it's embroidered." Sure enough, large, shaky letters spelled out "Lulu" in black thread, stark against the pink fabric.

"Did your mom make that for you?" Jade's heart broke. "Did she call you Lulu?"

Ears perked up. A whine escaped her throat. Lulu came to life, her tail slowly thumping against the cement floor.

"They've been calling you the wrong name this whole time? You poor thing." Jade was pretty sure she'd just found her spirit animal.

"Hi, Lulu." Andrew stretched out his hand for her to sniff as well. She rose from the bed, her pillow forgotten as she crossed the tiny space. Her tail picked up speed until she was nosing into their faces, sniffing intently.

The volunteer found them petting an eager wriggling dog that did not resemble the one she'd left them with at all.

"Oh, my gosh! How did you... Did you find your people?" She asked the dog, who responded with the first bark they'd heard from her and a doggie grin. "I have never seen her this excited. Holy crap."

"Can we put an application in for her?" Andrew asked as Jade wiped her eyes.

"Sure. But first, do you want to give her her dinner?" She lifted a silver dog bowl. "I usually have to put it right next to the bed to get her to eat."

"Give it here." Andrew opened the kennel door and laid the bowl down for Lulu.

They gave the dog one last pat each and explained they'd be back. Jade almost thought they'd have to sleep there when Lulu gave them the saddest puppy eyes she'd ever seen. But they had paperwork to fill out and a background check would have to be run on them before they could take her home.

After filling out the application, the volunteer assured them they would hear back in a couple of days. She also gave them some lists of recommended vets in the area and the food they used at the shelter, as well as information on how to get a license for the dog.

"I hate to leave her there," Jade gnawed on her thumbnail.

"Why don't we go to the pet store and get our supplies? I want to get that dog run set up before we bring her home."

"Do you think we'll get her?"

Andrew's voice was confident. "I'm almost positive. There's nothing in our backgrounds that would make them not approve us, and we definitely have the space. Plus, she's older and older dogs have a harder time getting adopted."

Jade grinned. "Let's go shopping."

And two days later, Lulu came home.

Thanks so much for reading The Geek Girl Squad: Jade! I would be honored if you'd leave a review so other romance readers can discover it, too!

Notes from Jasmine

Wow. I can't believe this crazy journey has come to an end. Writing a series has been such a learning experience and I love these girls so much, I don't think I'll ever be ready to let them go.

This book in particular took me on quite the emotional rollercoaster. And as I mentioned in the foreward, writing a trans heroine intimidated me. I didn't understand why I *had* to write Jade's story, until I saw this quote from Martin Buber.

> "This is the eternal origin of art that a human being confronts a form that wants to become a work through him. Not a figment of his soul but something that appears to the

soul and demands the soul's creative power."
- Martin Buber, *I and Thou*

I will be forever honored that she chose me.

I would like to acknowledge the brave trans women who put themselves out there in various publications that allowed me to educate myself enough to write this book: Janet Mock (*Redefining Realness* and *Surpassing Certainty*), May Peterson (specifically her fantasy romance, *The Calyx Charm*), Serena Sonoma (*Vice Magazine*), and Ashley Adamson on YouTube. Without them, this book would not be possible. Also many thanks to Kelsea, my sensitivity reader.

I'd also like to thank my critique partner, Hayley Green, even if you did make me go back and completely rewrite half the book (love you!). To my editor, Jenn, thank you for encouraging to write this series and subvert the annoying nerd girl makeover trope. My heartfelt thanks to my beta reader team, for your patience, especially when I throw multiple books at you back-to-back. For Erin and Dash, your fantastic illustrations brought these characters and settings to life. And of course, for my husband, who I know misses spending time with me when the characters demand my attention. You're the MVP, babe.

Next, I would never have published a damn thing if it weren't for these AuthorTubers: Dale. L. Roberts, Jenna Moreci, and Sasha Black.

Finally, to my readers: Thank you for going on this journey with me. I promise it's not over yet. You can expect to see some familiar faces in my next series, Hunt Security; a romantic suspense series focused on Nadia's older brothers. Until then, happy reading!

XOXO,

Jasmine

Also By Jasmine

For a current list of my available titles, scan the QR code below:

About the Author

I inherited my love of reading from my parents. As the daughter of two teachers, one of whom is also a librarian, I was the kid who walked out of the library with the maximum number of books each week, then walked back in the following week having read every single one. This would go on all summer long. When I could put pencil to paper, I started writing my own (terrible) kid's stories. Around age eight, I told my mom I wanted to be an author when I grew up, but she talked me out of it. She wanted me to have a stable career because of my poor health.

While I learned to manage my chronic condition through childhood, I also kept writing as a creative outlet. But when I grew up and turned my focus to my career, writing went by the wayside. The stories would not come again until quarantine in 2020 when trauma from the year before poured out of me in a cathartic story now known as *Roar for Me*. The decision to self-publish was an easy one. I consider each book its own work of art and I want to control not only what I write, but all the packaging, as well.

I write books I want to read. This means intelligent characters, happy-ever-afters, and no cheating. Adult contemporary romances with plenty of steam appeal to me the most. Music and pop culture are my biggest sources of inspiration. And I love to flip the script and surprise readers by putting a twist on their expectations.

Everyone deserves their own love story. I've always believed that. I want to develop a wide range of characters so everyone can relate to someone in one of my books. I especially love challenging gender expectations. And I hope my books will be an escape for readers, not just entertainment. When I'm not writing, I'm working in healthcare in my native Pittsburgh. Or you might find me crafting, baking sweet treats, or playing *Mario Kart* with my own nerdy love.

www.ingramcontent.com/pod-product-compliance
Lightning Source LLC
Chambersburg PA
CBHW021019310726
48969CB00006B/1463